"Touch me."

"Now? Here? Where anyone and everyone could see?"

Swallowing hard, Alyssa nodded. She didn't care. Was far beyond that point. Everyone acted crazy during Mardi Gras, she rationalized.

A tortured growl rumbled through the stranger's chest. The echo of it vibrated across her own skin.

Pouring every ounce of need into the connection, she met his devouring kiss and matched him. She wasn't content to simply acquiesce, but demanded a piece of him. Her teeth scraped across his bottom lip. Her tongue darted in to get a better taste.

Until he stopped, and pulled back.

"Last night I went home frustrated that you'd teased me, turned me on and then shut me out. Tonight it's my turn to walk away."

It hadn't just been a figment of her tired, deprived, overactive imagination.

"Unlike last night, I won't torture you with the possibility we might never finish what we started. Let me assure you...*we will.*"

Blaze®

Dear Reader,

The concept for *Captivate Me* came to me while I was listening to a fabulous Halestorm song. The idea of being invisible and ignored intrigued me.... Well, more the idea of finally being seen! We all want to be seen—to be important and wanted. After years of living in the shadows, that's exactly what Alyssa gets from Beckett. And what better time to lose her inhibitions and explore her inner vixen than the steamy days and sultry nights of Mardi Gras!

Beckett, on the other hand, prefers to stay behind the scenes, watching others let loose in his nightclubs. He's tired and a bit cynical, but when he catches sight of a beautiful stranger undressing in her window, he's intrigued. Alyssa surprises him, and for the first time in a long while makes him want to be a little bit wild—with her!

I hope you enjoy Beckett and Alyssa's story! I'd love to hear from you at kira@kirasinclair.com, or stop by and visit me on Facebook and Twitter.

Best wishes,

Kira

Captivate Me

—

Kira Sinclair

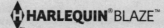
HARLEQUIN® BLAZE™

Recycling programs for this product may not exist in your area.

ISBN-13: 978-0-373-79791-2

CAPTIVATE ME

Printed in U.S.A.

ABOUT THE AUTHOR

Kira Sinclair is an award-winning author who writes emotional, passionate contemporary romances. Double winner of the National Readers' Choice Award, her first foray into writing fiction was for a high-school English assignment. Nothing could dampen her enthusiasm...not even being forced to read the love story aloud to the class. However, it definitely made her blush. Writing about striking, sexy heroes and passionate, determined women has always excited her. She lives out her own happily-ever-after with her amazing husband, their two beautiful daughters and a menagerie of animals on a small farm in North Alabama. Kira loves to hear from readers at www.kirasinclair.com.

Books by Kira Sinclair

HARLEQUIN BLAZE
415—WHISPERS IN THE DARK
469—AFTERBURN
588—CAUGHT OFF GUARD
605—WHAT MIGHT HAVE BEEN
667—BRING IT ON*
672—TAKE IT DOWN*
680—RUB IT IN*
729—THE RISK-TAKER
758—SHE'S NO ANGEL
766—THE DEVIL SHE KNOWS

*Island Nights

To get the inside scoop on Harlequin Blaze and its talented writers, be sure to check out blazeauthors.com.

Other titles by this author available in ebook format.
Don't miss any of our special offers. Write to us at the following address for information on our newest releases.

Harlequin Reader Service
U.S.: 3010 Walden Ave., P.O. Box 1325, Buffalo, NY 14269
Canadian: P.O. Box 609, Fort Erie, Ont. L2A 5X3

I'd like to dedicate this book to a group of people who have meant everything to me. I wouldn't be here without you guys. Thank you to everyone in Heart of Dixie for your support, encouragement and, of course, drinks at conference.

1

A PERFECT BLEND of the absurd and obscene. That described the French Quarter during Mardi Gras. Scantily clad women strolling beside men in cat costumes and stilts, all while evangelists screamed about the perils of sin.

Excess. Excitement. And that ever-present air of danger…because just about anything could—and did—happen.

Strangers rubbing against strangers because that was the only way through the wall-to-wall humanity. Heat and hedonism. Music, loud voices and raised laughter filling every available inch of space.

All around him, the party raged. But Beckett Kayne didn't care.

Leaning against the railing, he watched dispassionately as the crowd beneath the balcony swelled. Beside him Mason Westbrook, his best friend since childhood, held out several blinking LED necklaces. Shaking them enticingly, he yelled something crude.

Two women, wearing short, flared skirts and bustiers, giggled up at them with glassy-eyed interest. They clung together, no doubt keeping each other from falling flat on their wasted asses.

"You know what you have to do to get 'em," Mason taunted.

One of the women—and Beckett used the term loosely, because if they were a day over twenty-one he'd be damn surprised—shook her head slowly. Considering he owned a series of nightclubs scattered in major cities across the United States, he'd gotten pretty talented at spotting minors.

The brunette pouted. "We can't." Tugging at the edge of her top, she yelled, "It's too tight."

Mason simply grinned, his teeth flashing white through the dark night. "Then show me something else."

Moments like these, Beckett wondered why the hell he'd kept Mason in his life past the bonding years of their uninhibited carousing. Yes, there was a time when he would have been beside his friend, trying to coax the coeds into showing what the good Lord gave them.

But at thirty-two he was getting too old for this shit. Certainly too old for the doe-eyed girls on the street.

With a sense of disgust and inevitability, Beckett watched their heads go together as they whispered to each other, cutting quick glances up. After several moments they spun around. Beckett really hoped they were leaving but knew they probably weren't.

Instead, he watched them bend at the waist and flip up the edges of their skirts to show their practically naked rears.

Mason let out a wolf whistle and rained necklaces, gold coins and a handful of cheap trinkets down onto the street at their feet.

Tonight, the uncontrolled excess seriously bothered

Beckett. Or maybe that was just the bad mood he'd been fighting for the past few weeks. He was getting jaded.

Instead of growling something at Mason he'd most likely regret later, Beckett raised his glass and pulled a healthy swallow of expensive scotch into his mouth. It was smooth, and the welcome fire burning down his throat beat back the words threatening to break free.

He didn't want to be here. Had tried to tell Mason he'd be bad company, but his friend had guilted him into coming anyway. A private balcony party the Friday before Fat Tuesday, thrown by one of the partners in his firm, wasn't something to be missed.

But his head was firmly embedded in business and the way everything he wanted was slowly slipping through his fingers.

A dark scowl, an expression he'd been wearing all too often lately, pinched his brows. Beckett wasn't used to being…ignored and dismissed, but that was exactly what V&D Mobile Technology was doing.

Although not anymore. Not after tomorrow.

"Seriously, man, you're scaring off the chicks. Stop scowling. It's Mardi Gras," Mason yelled, as if the music, the people and the mask Beckett was currently wearing weren't enough for him to notice.

The air of wild debauchery, so palpable he could taste it on the back of his tongue, dark and sinfully sweet, was hard to ignore. Even if he would have liked to.

The girls on the street moved on, but Mason wasn't disappointed. Not when several feet away two more women, also decked out in feathered masks and barely stable enough to stay atop their skyscraper heels, pulled up their shirts and flashed their naked chests. A hailstorm of beads, accompanied by catcalls, landed at their feet.

Charming. Beckett looked away, disgust twisting hard in his gut. Shaking his head, he watched Mason scoot down the railing toward the women busy gathering the beads they'd exposed themselves to win.

Using Mason's distraction as a chance to finally slip away, Beckett moved farther into the shadows along the balcony. The big building was divided into expensive townhomes, making the space long and narrow. The balconies, on the second and third levels, curved around the front and all the way along the far side. Most everyone crowded near the street, so they could watch the people and party going on below.

Beckett just wanted a moment of peace to try and combat the headache threatening to balloon into a migraine. Settling his back against the rough brick, he propped a single foot on the intricate metal railing in front of him and closed his eyes. A deep breath and another healthy swallow of scotch had some of the knots unwinding from between his shoulder blades.

He could still hear the noise from the street, but the side balcony wrapped around into a controlled-access alley. During Mardi Gras, without fences—and sometimes with—every square inch of real estate was covered with humanity. But this building was pricey enough to have very good security—high fences, electronic locks and surveillance cameras. With a practiced eye, Beckett had noticed the expensive recording equipment.

The alley was empty, filled with nothing but shadows, trash cans and a black cat that stared at him with wide, yellow eyes. He was enjoying the muted solitude, gearing up for his inevitable return to the decadence, when a light snapped on in an apartment across the alley.

It startled him. That was the only reason he looked. But once he did…he couldn't tear his gaze away.

The balcony he was standing on was higher than the windows he was staring straight into, which meant he was looking slightly down into the room.

A bedroom.

A woman's bedroom.

Blue, green and purple light scattered across the space from a stained-glass lamp on the bedside table. Shadows chased across pale green walls and smooth, dark floors. Heavy furniture, the solid kind that carried age and history, filled the room.

A four-poster bed occupied most of the space with gleaming golden wood and an inviting cloud of fluffy jewel-toned pillows. Appealing and comfortable, the whole room looked like a sumptuous invitation he wanted to accept.

But that really wasn't what had his gaze glued.

She stood framed by the window. A soft radiance from the lamp slipped across her body. It lit her from behind, painting her in an ethereal splash of color that made her seem dreamy and tragic and somehow unreal.

Maybe that's why he kept watching. Logically, he realized he was intruding, but there was something about her….

Her head drooped as if she was too tired to hold it up. Her shoulders slumped. He watched them rise and fall on the kind of heavy breath that was more ragged sigh than actual exhalation. Without even hearing it, the sigh shot straight through him.

Until that moment she'd been facing away from him, but she turned slightly, giving him her profile. And she was gorgeous. Little pug nose, elegant jawline, lush lips.

Her hair curled over her shoulder in a wave of brown and gold that caught the light and reflected it. His hands itched to sweep it away so that he could run his fingers down the curve of her throat.

Her eyelids slid closed and her head tipped back. Exhaustion was stamped into every line of her body, but that didn't detract from her allure. In fact, it made Beckett want to reach out and hold her more. To take her weight and the exhaustion on himself.

Her hands drifted slowly up her body, settling at the top button of her blouse. With sure fingers, she popped it open. And another. And another. The edge of her hot-red bra came into view, revealing the swell of enticing breasts, a beautiful, pale expanse of skin.

Tension snapped through Beckett's body. Perhaps the hedonistic pressure of the night had gotten to him after all. Because, even as his brain was screaming at him to avert his gaze and give her the privacy she obviously thought she had, he couldn't do it.

Especially as her nimble fingers kept going, giving him more. Suddenly restless, he couldn't stay still. His muscles twitched, pulsed. Three minutes ago he'd been nursing the beginnings of a headache. Now the ache had moved much farther south.

It had been a very long time since any woman had pulled this kind of immediate physical reaction from him. Spending most of his nights surrounded by inebriated females on the prowl, he'd become a little jaded. After years of being immersed in the cat-and-mouse games, day in and day out, he was long past tired of being a player—or played.

Perhaps it was her air of innocence that not even the windowpane and ten feet of alley could camouflage. Or the fact that she wasn't playing at anything right now. She was simply herself—unconsciously sensual.

Shifting, Beckett dropped his foot and settled his waist against the hard edge of the railing. Why, he had no idea. It wasn't as though he could span the space between them. Not really. At least, not with anything other than his gaze.

He wanted to be the one uncovering her soft skin. Undressing her slowly, like a present he'd been waiting all year to receive. To run his fingers over her body. Hear the hitch of her breath when he discovered a sensitive spot. Watch her pupils dilate in response to his touch.

The need was staggering, compelling. It scared him. But not enough to turn away. He wasn't certain anything could have forced him to do that.

Maybe it was his movement that caught her attention, or the weight of his heated gaze finally penetrating her preoccupation. But suddenly her head snapped up and she looked straight into his eyes.

He watched the movement of her startled gasp, the swell of her breasts as they surged against the cups of her lace-edged bra. Her fingers stilled midmotion. Surprise, embarrassment and anger flitted across her face before finally settling into something darker and a hell of a lot more sinful.

Her head cocked to the side, considering.

She hadn't screeched down the place. Or slammed the blinds shut.

Without breaking eye contact, Beckett relaxed against the wall, as if settling in for the show, and crossed his arms over his chest. Lifting a single eyebrow, he dared her to keep going and held his breath, praying she would.

It was late. The craziness that was the last weekend

before Fat Tuesday permeated the atmosphere. Maybe that spell was working them both.

Heartbreakingly slowly, she turned, giving him a full frontal view. The fingers that had gone still began to move again, making quick work of the few buttons that were left. The edges of her shirt fluttered open. His eyes sharpened, trying to see every minute detail of her body through the distance and the night.

Flat stomach, gorgeous expanse of perfect, creamy skin. He registered the slight pink tinge that swept up her chest and throat. Was it embarrassment, arousal or both?

Tugging each cuff at her wrists, she held her arms wide open and let the gauzy material slither against her skin. Down, down, down, until it puddled on the floor at her feet.

The cups of her bra sat low, barely containing the curve of her breasts. He could see the top arch of her are-olae, a deep, dark pink. The color of raspberries. Would she be just as sweet and tart against his tongue?

Lace edged the top of her bra. He imagined it tickling across her sensitive nipples. Two teeny, tiny straps, look-ing as if they might snap at any moment, curved over her shoulders and strained against the heavy weight of her breasts. Never in his life had Beckett wanted so desper-ately for fabric to break.

Then she spun away. A growling protest was out of his mouth, and he'd taken a step forward before he real-ized she wasn't stopping, simply giving him her back.

Heavy lines of ink curled across her skin. Over her ribs, black, blue and purple twisted together into a pic-ture. He couldn't see all of it, but enough to get the gist. Delicate wings, ethereal body, flowing hair. Just like her, the lithe fairy was turned away, showing only her back and bowed head.

For some reason, the picture she'd permanently placed on her skin made his chest ache. It reminded him of how she'd looked when she'd first walked into the room, exhausted and a little tragic.

Before he could follow that thread of thought, her arms reached behind her, blocking out his view of her ink. Her palms slipped down, smoothing her skirt. The material clung to her body, hugging the curve of her ass in a way that made his hands itch to do the same. Because he couldn't, Beckett curled his fingers into fists.

The skirt pulled in, following the contours of her hips and narrowing to skim her thighs. The hem hit just above her knees, a perfectly respectable length. But that didn't stop him from feeling sorry for every poor bastard who had to work with her, watch her prance around in that skirt and know his chances of getting beneath it were slim.

She took a single step forward, opening the slit that lined up perfectly with the seam of her thighs. This time, the groan Beckett bit back had nothing to do with fear that she was going to stop.

The slit ended near the tops of her thighs, hinting at what lay beneath. That hint was torture. Because, with the slit held open by her position, all he could see were shadows promising him so much more than she was giving.

Beckett's mouth went dry and then flooded with moisture. He wanted to taste her. To discover the musky scent of her arousal and press his face right there into those shadows.

Twisting, she set her pointy little chin on her shoulder

and watched him as her fingers tugged at the zipper. Her hands eased the material down, inch by excruciating inch, revealing the scorching-red panties that matched her bra.

Satin and lace, the boyshorts covered her sweet curves. Something about them was both chaste and tantalizing. Like her, a contradiction. Adorably innocent yet devilishly tempting.

His eyes had been trained so intently on her rounded curves that it took him several moments to notice she was wearing thigh highs beneath that skirt.

Dear God in heaven.

Lace wrapped around the expanse of each thigh, cutting in and holding on. He could practically feel the silky texture of them against his palms, rubbing up and down his ribs as her thighs gripped him. Beckett swallowed. Hard. And the tiny, taunting smile that played across her lips told him she knew exactly the reaction she was pulling from him.

Dammit. It had been a very long time since he'd let a woman have the upper hand. How had this one managed it? With ten feet and a pane of glass between them.

When she walked several feet away from him, he got an unbelievably amazing view of her entire body. Killer legs he could imagine around his waist. Hips that swayed seductively. The firm curve of a good ass. The curl of ink, proof that she wasn't as buttoned up as her outward appearance suggested. Long expanse of elegant spine, riotous curls begging to have a man's hands twined in them and holding her close.

This woman was a siren. That's all there was to it.

Lifting a single foot to the bench at the end of her bed, she plastered her body down the length of her thigh to lean over and unbuckle the heel still strapped on. Her breasts swayed, straining against the material barely holding them in.

Pain and need and craving pounded through him, settling so deep in his bones he was afraid the ache would never leave.

Her right foot was on the bench angling her body away from him. Flipping him a look over her shoulder and from beneath her lashes, she watched him even as she rolled the stocking carefully down her leg.

Her body swayed gently, the lace at the bottom of her panties creeping higher to give him an alluring glimpse of more. The metal teeth of his zipper bit into the straining length of his erection. He was light-headed from all the blood rushing to his groin.

He couldn't remember a single time when he'd wanted a woman so much. Beckett hadn't touched her and didn't even know her name, but that didn't seem to matter. There was something about her that…drew him.

All he could think of was tasting her skin. Hearing the sound of her moans, her sharp inhale of breath when he finally pushed home, filling her up and bringing them both unbearable ecstasy.

His hands clenched around the railing, desperately needing an anchor to keep him from slipping entirely into the fantasy.

Devouring her with his eyes, Beckett watched as she straightened and moved back to the window. Her gaze burned as she studied him. Not just with lust, but something more. He felt the pressure of it licking through his blood. It was as if she could see beneath his skin. Recognized just how alone he was, even constantly surrounded by other people.

Because she was just as lonely.

He expected her to stop when she reached the window. Maybe drop her bra to the floor. Or crook her finger and silently tell him to come finish what they'd both started.

What he was too far gone to anticipate was for her to press her breasts right up against the window. The movement tugged at the already precarious edge of her bra giving him a peek at her nipples. Tiny buds hard and tight with the same desire running rampant through his own body. There was no denying she was just as turned on as he was.

He could read it in the desperate glow of her eyes, the flush of her skin and the languid, liquid way her body moved.

Her arms stretched wide out to her sides. She undulated, rolling her hips and ribs and spine in a way that begged him to touch.

And then the blind snapped down between them.

SAGGING AGAINST THE wall beside the window now covered by the wide slats of her plantation blinds, Alyssa Vaughn let her body slide down. The polished hardwood floor was cold on her rear when it hit, but she welcomed the shock. Maybe it would cool the sizzling tremble running rampant through her body.

She dropped her head to her knees and screwed her eyes shut.

What the hell had she been thinking?

She hadn't. That was the problem.

The moment her eyelids closed, her overheated mind conjured up the image of *him* again. A beautiful man with dark, intense eyes that had scraped across her body with a blazing heat, leaving her breathless. Half of his face obscured by a brightly colored mask.

His body had been just as hidden beneath the dark lines of an expensive suit. But she'd known, instinctively, the fire and strength he harbored. Could see it in the flex of long, tapered fingers and bulge of thigh muscles against smooth fabric.

Dangerously elegant. Like the sleekest jungle cat, beautiful in its power, but deadly when provoked.

The man had stirred some force inside her. The way he'd watched her, gaze sharp and exquisitely intense, focused on every miniscule movement. As though there was nothing in the world for him right then except what she was showing. Nothing more important than what they were sharing.

Excitement and something much more dangerous flashed beneath her skin. A craving that went deeper than mere physical satisfaction. A need long buried. A hope long denied.

Sucking a hard breath through her teeth, Alyssa forced her arms to relax and drop away from their tight hold around her body. She raised her head and let it clunk against the wall. Staring up at the ceiling she'd painted a pale heather gray, she focused on breathing, slow and steady.

No harm done. She'd stopped before going too far. Before letting free that wild piece of herself she kept locked down tight. Always ignored.

A bra and boyshorts were no more revealing than most bathing suits. She hadn't done anything wrong. So why was she struggling with a sickening mixture of guilt, exhilaration and dismay?

He had no idea who she was. It had been late, dark, with only a lamp on for light. He'd been wearing a mask and was ten feet away, lodged in the shadows. They could collide on the street and never know each other.

A moment of insanity. Mardi Gras madness. A release from the stress and pressure she'd been dealing with all day.

It was over. Or, at least, it would be once she dealt with the hum of residual sexual energy lodged squarely between her thighs.

And if, in the throes of passion when her defenses were weak, she imagined his heated gaze sweeping across her body, watching intently as she finished what he'd started, there was no way anyone else would ever know that—especially him.

2

THEY WERE DESPERATE. And that's just how Beckett wanted them.

Unfortunately, so was he, although, even as he strode into their plush offices, he had no intention of letting V&D know that.

He needed their app. Would do anything to own it. It was the game changer. Something that would take his nightclubs from simply successful to infamous. Like Studio 54, he wanted Exposed to become a household name, the kind whispered with awe and envy.

He craved the notoriety, money and irrefutable proof that he was finally successful, his life stable. The familiar desperation tasted bitter in his mouth.

What a difference fourteen years could make. At eighteen he'd been kicked out of the massive mansion he'd called home, and the whiplash with which he'd lost everything had hurt. But not nearly as much as realizing his father didn't give a damn about him.

Without a penny or any discernible skills, he'd floundered, imposing on friends, sleeping on couches, carrying what little his father had let him take in a garbage bag. But it had become clear that wasn't a long-term solution.

He'd had no place to live. Had never held a job. It might not have sounded like a sob story to anyone else, but going a few days without anything to eat after having every meal provided on gold-rimmed plates had been a hell of a shock to the system.

The fake ID he'd used to get into clubs had been useful in convincing the owner of a seedy nightclub to give him a chance. He'd started out slinging drinks, but soon realized that wasn't going to be enough.

Six months later he was managing the place, his natural charm and leadership skills taking over. Splitting the profits with a drunk who wasn't coherent enough to realize what he was giving up hadn't exactly been the stuff of lifelong dreams, but Beckett had socked away every penny until he'd had enough to open his own place.

It'd taken four years, but a year after he actually turned legal he opened the first Exposed deep in the New Orleans Warehouse District. Funky and eclectic, it had appealed to a wide range of people.

Two years later came the club in New York. Then L.A., Nashville, Chicago and Seattle. He now owned twelve locations. But that wasn't enough.

Part of him wondered if there would ever be enough. If success and security could wipe out those first few years of desperation.

Especially when his father delighted in reminding him just how much of a disappointment and failure he'd once been. Or that the money he'd made since was on the back of something lurid and common.

As if the man hadn't come from humble beginnings himself. His father was a self-made billionaire. And a ruthless asshole, like a lion eating his young to protect his power position within the pride.

Beckett didn't care how he made his mark, though. It didn't bother him that he did it by selling alcohol and providing a dark place where inhibitions dropped and people hooked up.

Sex and sensationalism sold. Which was exactly why he needed V&D's new social media app. Having a dozen Exposed locations was great. But allowing anyone with a smartphone to feel as if they were at his clubs…that would open his revenue stream up to every city in the country. Hell, in the world. Billions of people dropping in to watch and interact.

However, V&D refused to even entertain his offers.

Which just pissed him off.

It had been a long time since someone had been stupid enough to disrespect him to his face, but that was what V&D was doing. Treating his blood, sweat and tears like the ten-year-old banished to the kiddie table at Christmas. Dismissing him as if he was insignificant. That, more than anything, was what had lodged beneath his skin, itching and burning.

Well, they'd surely realized that was far from the truth by now. He was more than significant. He had them by the balls.

They wouldn't listen to reason, so he'd simply take what he wanted.

He was going to enjoy watching them squirm. And while that would certainly be entertaining, what he really hoped to gain from this meeting was an understanding of what he'd done to piss them off so much they'd excluded him from the negotiations in the first place.

He hated to be in the dark. That's when you were open

and vulnerable. Beckett did not like being exposed. And the irony wasn't lost on him at all.

Now V&D were scrambling, and Beckett was going to enjoy sitting back and watching the show. This would be fun.

He grasped the handle of the conference room door and his heart rate kicked. He embraced the physical evidence of his anticipation, letting it free for just a moment. A smile flickered across his lips. Then, completely in control, he wiped his expression clean.

Striding forward with confidence, he raked his gaze across the conference table and the people already waiting. And he nearly stumbled.

Blood, adrenaline and a bone-deep craving flooded his body. Every muscle went solid, straining against his skin and the need to reach across the table, grasp the woman staring at him and kiss the hell out of her.

Although the daggers she currently had pointed at him said that probably wouldn't go over well.

Beckett's years of harsh control served him well. Shaking his head, he pulled out the chair opposite the gathered contingent and settled against the soft leather surface. Leaning back, he let the chair tip off center and take his weight, his body lax and comfortable.

Scraping the group with a practiced, sharp smile that was all teeth and challenge, he waited to see what their first move would be.

He'd been looking forward to this meeting all morning, but suddenly it had gone from entertaining to downright thrilling.

Because sitting across from him, elegant, cold and seriously pissed off, was the last person he'd ever expected to see.

The woman was far from the tech geek he'd anticipated. While he'd been doing research on both of the partners, the V in V&D had remained a mystery. In an age of social media, she hadn't had a Facebook, Twitter or Google+ account. Which had struck him as weird, considering she was the brains behind a company poised to explode into the highly competitive tech market.

Hell, she was selling a social media app and didn't have a single social media account. No photographs or videos of her drunken college days on YouTube. According to rumor, she valued her privacy, preferring her lab, computers and code to actual human interaction.

He'd half prepared himself for some shy, mousy thing with pale skin and eyes bloodshot from staring at flickering screens too long.

Instead, her pale-green gaze was definitely not foggy or distracted. It was intelligent, angry and trained solely on him.

A blouse the same shade as her eyes was buttoned up tight. A single strand of gleaming pearls nestled against the hollow of her throat. The long, lush hair was swept up into a tight twist, bangs feathering across her forehead.

She was clearly the prim and proper businesswoman ready to plunge into shark-infested waters...and win. And maybe, if fate hadn't intervened, the ruse would have worked.

But he knew her secrets.

He'd seen her naked skin, that heartbreaking tattoo and her sexy lingerie just last night, framed in the lonely window of a French Quarter apartment.

ALYSSA WATCHED HIM stride into the room, powerful, commanding and utterly confident in his own skin. She'd braced for the impact, but it hadn't done much good.

The moment he entered it felt as if all the oxygen had been sucked from the room. Her lungs deflated, leaving her gasping for breath.

It had been years since she'd seen the man, although their single encounter had left a lasting impression. Not just on her psyche, but on her life.

Although she'd bet next year's profits he didn't have the first clue who she was…or that he'd once had his tongue down her throat and his hand up her skirt.

Or that he'd humiliated her.

She'd been sixteen and upset from a fight with Bridgett and her father before a friend had picked her up for a party. Her stepmother had accused her of things she hadn't done—drugs, drinking, seeing an older guy. Without a second thought, her father had believed every word his wife fed him.

That betrayal had hurt. She'd arrived at the party hell-bent on letting loose. If she was going to be painted with the brush then she should at least enjoy the experience. That first beer had tasted terrible, but by the fourth she'd no longer cared about anything.

She'd been thoroughly blitzed by the time Lindsey had pointed out a group of older boys who'd graduated from their exclusive private prep school several years before. Alyssa had noticed Beckett Kayne immediately. Who wouldn't? He was gorgeous in a wickedly danger-ous kind of way that appealed to the rebellious streak she was tired of denying.

Without the liquid courage she probably never would have walked up to him, grabbed his face and kissed the hell out of him. What she hadn't been prepared for was her immediate, all-consuming response. Or how quickly he took control, backing her into a corner and letting his hands roam across her body.

They didn't dance or talk, just skipped straight to trying to find an unoccupied room. But somewhere through the haze of alcohol, groping and sparkling heat, Alyssa remembered she needed to tell him she was a virgin. The moment the slurred words left her mouth everything changed.

Beckett vaulted away from her as if she'd suddenly developed the plague. On top of the other emotional upheaval of the night, that loss had felt like a kick in the gut.

It wasn't until the next day that she truly understood the depth of Beckett's duplicity. One of his friends let it slip that he'd had his eye on her all night…not because he was interested, but because he was desperate for money, she was young and her father was loaded.

Alyssa bit back a bitter chuckle. If only he'd known he was wasting his time, even the little he'd invested. Her father might have been rich as Croesus, but she sure as hell hadn't been. Wasn't. Maybe never would be. Although, money had never really mattered to her.

He'd left her there, humiliated, drunk and alone. She'd been forced to call her father to come pick her up. Ignoring the tear tracks on her cheeks, he and her stepmother had lit into her. Bridgett had ranted about what a bad influence she was on her half sister, Mercedes.

And there was nothing she could say.

From that night on, any hope she'd ever had of repairing her relationship with her father had crumbled to dust.

But that had been years ago, and until Kayne's name had come across her desk, attached to an intent to bid notice for the Watch Me app, she'd thought she was long over the experience.

Oh, how wrong she'd been. Just his name had sent anger, humiliation and something much more sinful washing across her skin. There was no way in hell she'd do business with the man and she'd said as much to her partner, Mitch Dornigan.

They might be equal owners of V&D, but he hadn't protested or questioned her snap decision. In the weeks since, her anger hadn't dissipated. In fact, it had only increased, especially with the man's latest stunt. She wanted to reach across the conference table and scratch the smug expression right off his face.

Unfortunately, that didn't stop her from reacting to him. Just the sight of his powerful, suit-clad body had energy humming through her bones, pure electricity. Her pulse skittered, her mouth went dry and her palms started to sweat.

God, she hated that Beckett Kayne had this kind of primal effect on her. She was a strong, independent and intelligent woman. So why, the moment he walked into her sphere of existence, did her brain go haywire and her body revolt?

The simple answer was that the man was inherently sensual in a dark and dangerous sort of way. Even more so now than back then. Any living, breathing female would respond to him. The problem was, he knew exactly the effect he had and wasn't afraid to use it. Beckett Kayne had a reputation for being ruthless, using whatever advantage he was given.

She had no intention of giving him any more by letting him know just how he affected her.

His thick brown hair made a woman want to grab and take hold. His moody blue eyes were consuming and observant. Rumor had it that he liked to watch, from a room high above the floor of his clubs.

An unwanted shiver snaked down her spine. Alyssa shook it off. Now was not the time. She had to get a grip. The man was here to destroy her business, something she'd spent the past two years building. She'd be damned if she was going to let him. She needed her mind clear and her faculties focused.

He wore a precisely tailored business suit. The material was expensive and skimmed across his body in a way that highlighted the lean muscles and tight build hidden beneath. It was a far cry from the tight jeans, frayed at the hem, and skintight black T-shirt he'd worn the first time they met.

Then he'd looked like an outlaw. An air of danger had clung to his skin along with the scent of alcohol, musk and something purely male. But that wasn't what had drawn her. Beneath that there'd been a…vulnerability. A misery she recognized, understood and, for some strange reason, wanted to soothe.

Apparently that had been a lie, as well.

She wanted to think the business suit was an improvement, but somehow not even that facade could hide the edge of savagery, the tiger pacing lazily behind iron bars. You just knew if he ever broke free, that deceptive drowsiness would disappear and he'd rip your head off.

Beckett Kayne moved with that same kind of powerful, predatory grace.

Biting back a growl of frustration—at herself—Alyssa watched him drop into the chair across from her and cut a smile over her people. Two seats down, Deirdre sighed, the soft gush of air difficult to misinterpret. He hadn't even opened his mouth and she was already mesmerized.

The one saving grace was that Kayne didn't even bother to look in Deirdre's direction. His eyes were trained unflinchingly on her.

A few seconds stretched into thirty, sixty and then more. Alyssa fought the heavy weight of silence. The pressure built, as if her insides were frantically moving while she sat perfectly still, waiting for him to make the first move. The sensation was unnerving...almost as much as Beckett Kayne's scrutiny.

Something wicked flashed in his eyes, but before she could blink it was gone. Tingles raced across her skin. Slowly, the most amazing smile stretched his mouth. Wide, knowing and enigmatic, for some reason it made fear spin deep in the pit of her belly.

"Ms. Vaughn, wonderful to finally meet you."

The warm, throaty rumble of his voice didn't help to quell the churning. In fact, it made it worse. There was an edge to his words, some deeper meaning that made her muscles tense.

Could he actually remember?

No, surely not.

"I'm afraid I can't say the same, Mr. Kayne." Grinding her teeth together, Alyssa struggled to keep her emotions in check and tone civil. "I don't appreciate the position you've put us in."

She'd hoped to see a flash of regret. Or maybe just something that proved the man had a heart. To her surprise, instead of dimming, his smile morphed. His eyelids went heavy, dropping into a lazy, sensual squint. His mouth crooked, pulling higher on one side. Some might say it was a flaw, his one imperfection. But after all these years it was the thing she remembered most.

It made him human. Attainable. Real.

Once her gaze was snagged, Alyssa fought to force it away from his lips. And failed. It was the only reason she noticed the telltale twitch of humor.

"You gave me no choice, Ms. Vaughn, by ignoring my requests to do business together."

Blowing out a sound of frustration, Alyssa couldn't stop her voice from rising. "Perhaps you should invest in a dictionary, Mr. Kayne. It might fill in some of the gaps your lack of education has apparently left. Not giving you the answer you want isn't the same as ignoring you."

His lips flattened into a compressed line. Disappointment clawed at her. *That* she did ignore. Or tried.

"We weren't interested in doing business with you."

"Yes, you made that abundantly clear, although I have no idea why. The problem is you made that decision while simultaneously leaving yourselves vulnerable. I've never been the kind of man to walk away from an open invitation."

Probably sensing just how close she was to losing it, Mitch stepped in before she said something that would derail any possibility of finding a reasonable solution to the situation.

"Taking out that loan was hardly an invitation."

Kayne shrugged his shoulders, the motion smooth and negligent. "That's the problem with doing business with friends. Taking out a private loan with a personal acquaintance instead of a bank is always risky. Less legal oversight governing the contract."

Alyssa's jaw ached from the pressure to keep her mouth from overriding her brain. She'd had plenty of practice swallowing her words, but for some reason the ones she swallowed now were more bitter than any others.

They'd tried to get a conventional loan and none of

the banks would back them. Why would they, when the business was already in the red? The bank's algorithms and number crunchers couldn't take their upcoming success into account. They were weeks away from a huge influx of capital when their first app sold. And they had another that would be ready within the next two months.

Both she and Mitch had already been tapped out, savings gone and mortgaged to the gills. They'd only needed a few months' operating capital to make it through, though, and everything would be fine. They'd been so close....

When Mitch had suggested going to a family friend for the money, someone he trusted and had known for most of his life, it had seemed an obvious solution. Sure, it carried more risk, but they'd felt fairly safe and confident in taking that chance.

Hindsight was definitely twenty-twenty.

Apparently, the connection Mitch had counted on had been outweighed by blind greed. According to their sources, Beckett had purchased their loan for almost a fourth more than the face value of the contract.

They were supposed to have six months to pay off the loan. More than enough time to bridge the gap. However, Kayne had decided to activate an escape clause, which allowed him to call the loan due at any point during the term. And he was pulling the trigger.

They had less than two weeks to come up with a huge chunk of change or Beckett Kayne would legally own V&D, including all their intellectual property—specifically, the app he so desperately wanted. She had no intention of letting him have Watch Me.

Not only would it gall her to lose the technology to the

man, but they desperately needed the funds from selling the app to keep V&D moving forward.

A few days ago, Alyssa would have said there was no way she could hate Beckett Kayne any more than she already did. She'd have been wrong about that, too. Frustration and desperation warred inside her.

Her hands clenched into tight fists beneath the table as she tried to reign in her emotional turmoil before it bubbled up and spilled out all over the place like a destructive, scorching flow of lava.

"You can't tell me that in all your years as a businessman, you never took a calculated risk?"

His churning gaze zeroed back on her. "Of course. The difference is, I made damn sure the reward was worth it."

Realizing this line of discussion was getting them nowhere, Alyssa cut to the chase. "What do you want, Kayne?"

"I would have thought that was obvious."

A frustrated sound buzzed in the back of her throat. "I'd rather you spell it out for me so there are no misunderstandings or false assumptions."

The smile fell away, taking the facade with it and leaving behind a piercing expression that had a tremor racing through her body. For the first time since he'd walked in the door, Alyssa felt like maybe she was getting a true glimpse of the man. The problem was it scared her spitless. Beckett Kayne was a bloodthirsty animal with his prey clearly in his sights.

"Watch Me. I want it. Exclusively."

"You're making a mistake."

"I seriously doubt it."

Alyssa crossed her arms beneath her breasts and stared him down. "I assure you, you are. You think you've got us backed into a corner. You're already counting your win. Don't forget we still have time to come up with the funds."

His shoulders rose and fell on a negligent shrug that had her teeth clacking together. She didn't have the luxury of reacting, not if she wanted to save her company and the work she'd poured her heart and soul into for the past eighteen months.

"Call off your attack dogs. Get your offer together and let us review it along with the others we're expecting in next week. We'll even give you a few extra days if you need them."

"Why would I do that, Ms. Vaughn? Long before you can formalize any offers and arrange payment I'll have what I want. For the bargain price of a few months of your operating capital *I'll* own not just the app, but your entire company."

Dread flooded her mouth, it tasted bitter and vile, but she choked back her reaction. She would not let Beckett Kayne see her sweat.

"I will not let you destroy V&D. We'll have the money in time, and when we do any chance you had for procuring the app disappears."

Something sharp flashed through his blue-gray eyes. "You've made it clear I have no chance anyway. You forced me to play dirty, Ms. Vaughn. You don't have the luxury of crying foul now that you're the one sitting there covered in muck."

Alyssa wheezed out a breath. But she refused to let his words derail her. She leaned across the table, closing the space between them. "I'm giving you one chance to do the right thing, Beckett. We both know calling that loan due four months early is a dirty move."

Surprising her, Kayne matched her movements, leaning against the edge of the table and deep into her personal space. His stare was hard and indecipherable.

"It isn't a dirty move. It's a smart move. You strike me as an intelligent women, Ms. Vaughn. Something tells me you're perfectly aware of my reputation. Do I look like the kind of man who'd care even if it was?"

Silence and tension crackled between them, making everything inside her contract.

Something hard and hedonistic glittered in his eyes. The corners of his mouth twitched. Her own gaze dropped to the movement. But once there…she couldn't look away.

His lips were lush, perfect, with a hint of harshness. Not the kind of man who'd be soft and safe in bed. She wanted to press her mouth tight to his and find out. Would he devour her? Nibble and tease? Demand her surrender or leave her drowning in a sensual haze?

She sucked in a sharp breath, the sound exploding into the quiet room. Everyone heard it. They had to, and no doubt knew exactly what it meant…that she'd been waylaid by the pull of Beckett Kayne.

With a satisfied smirk on his face, Kayne dropped back into his chair.

"I am doing the right thing, Ms. Vaughn. I'm acquiring the cutting-edge technology that will take my company worldwide, by any means necessary and open to me. I learned a long time ago—the hard way, I might add—that there are no friends in business. It's every man, or woman, for himself. This world can be cruel. You were bound to learn that lesson at some point. I'd like to say I'm sorry I had to be involved in the education, but that would be a lie." His stormy eyes flashed, pinning her in place. "I've enjoyed matching wits with you too much to regret the experience."

From the far end of the table, Deirdre made a small choking sound. Mitch leaned forward, body tense and hands splayed across the table as if he were about to vault over and rip into Kayne.

Alyssa stopped him, curling her fingers around his wrist to hold her business partner in place. Beckett's gaze dropped to her hand, his eyes narrowing.

His sharp, steady gaze returned to hers, and his voice lowered into a dangerous growl, "Let me assure you, Ms. Vaughn, I always get what I want."

Alyssa's lungs seized, stealing her ability to respond. Not that she'd have had much opportunity. Surging to his feet, Beckett Kayne ended the discussion long before she was through, disappearing out the door.

Beside her, Mitch snarled. Deirdre sighed, slumping back into her chair.

And Alyssa just sat there, dumbfounded. Her body was a jumble of useless reactions. Her skin tingled, her heart thumped, her skin flushed with swelling temper. She had no outlet for any of it.

Why did it feel as if he meant to own much more than her company?

3

THE DOOR CLICKED shut behind Kayne. Every molecule of tension left the room right along with him. Apparently that tension had been holding her up, because the second it was gone Alyssa's body slumped into a boneless mess.

What were they going to do?

There was always her stepmother. Just the thought of the perfectly coiffed, hypercritical, manipulative woman had Alyssa letting out a groan.

Sucking in a hard breath, she let her head drop, not even trying to stop the sharp pain as her skull clunked heavily against the edge of the table. Because that pain was better than the inevitable agony that resulted whenever she ventured into the same zip code as her stepmother, she did it again. And again.

"Jesus, Lys, stop it," Mitch said beside her, slapping his palm in front of her so she'd hit him instead of the table.

Her forehead smacked into the warmth of his hand and instead of going back for more, she rolled against him. Back and forth, as if shaking her head would allow her to deny everything that was happening and make it all disappear.

With a sigh, Alyssa said, "Deirdre, can you leave us for a bit?"

Pretending wouldn't help the situation, even if it was tempting to run away and lock herself into the comforting solitude of her workroom. Her computers never yelled or criticized or ignored. They were there when she needed them, uncomplicated and nonjudgmental.

But she was far from the emotionally damaged girl she'd once been. She'd spent years fighting for her self-confidence, to figure out who she was and where she belonged in the world. And she'd be damned if anyone—especially Beckett Kayne—sent her back to that dark, lonely place.

The warmth of Mitch's hand settled between her shoulder blades. Just…there. As he always was. Not for the first time, she wondered why she couldn't be attracted to him. But she wasn't and never would be. With Mitch it had always been easy and comfortable. No tension. He didn't make her skin tighten with anticipation or her heart flutter with awareness. He was the protective older brother she'd never had and always needed.

"We'll figure this out, Lys. I promise."

Twisting her head, she looked up at him, forcing a sad smile to her lips.

Mitch had always been the one shining light when she'd needed it most. Whenever she started to feel so thin and invisible everyone could surely see straight through her, he'd forced her back into existence. He wouldn't let her disappear into herself.

He'd saved the girl she'd been and given her the space and support she'd needed to become the woman she was.

She owed him everything, including whatever it would cost her to fix this mess.

Bridgett, her stepmother, was calculating and ruthless. Alyssa had no idea how her father had never known just how cold his wife could be. No, that wasn't true. He never knew because Bridgett didn't want him to see. She was pregnant less than three months after their wedding, and from the moment Mercedes had come into the world Bridgett had made sure her father doted on his youngest child. Spoiled her. Gave her everything, most especially his attention and love.

Alyssa had become a fifth wheel, completely unnecessary and unwanted.

By the time Alyssa hit her teens, Bridgett had convinced her father she was a poor reflection on the Vaughn name and her father's pristine reputation.

Alyssa couldn't remember the moment she realized her father despised her. The seed had simply grown until it blossomed into painful understanding. She was a constant reminder of her mother, who'd chosen to run off with a penniless mechanic rather than remain in the opulent world and stifling perfection Alyssa's father had demanded. Transferring his rage to his daughter had been easy.

He'd never hurt her, at least not physically. It might have been easier if he had. Then maybe someone else would have recognized her pain.

Bridgett had gotten exactly what she wanted—almost all of her husband's money. When he'd died four years ago he'd left everything to her. Everything except enough for Alyssa to put a nice down payment on her apartment in the Quarter. She never would have been able to afford the mortgage without it.

The irony was that she hadn't wanted his money. What she'd craved was a father who loved and doted on her the way he obviously cared about Mercedes. But that unfulfilled dream died right along with him.

She could ask Bridgett for the money. Alyssa's eyes closed on a convulsive gesture of dread. And her stepmother would give it to her just so she could hold it up as evidence of Alyssa's failure. Her stomach rolled with loathing.

"Don't even think about it," Mitch warned, his dark brown eyes flashing. "There's no way I'm letting you do it."

"Do what?" she asked listlessly.

"Going to the Stepford Witch is a last resort."

Mitch knew her so well. She hadn't even had to voice the option for him to know exactly the hell her head had gone to.

"Uh, I think we're there, Mitch."

His fingers hardened, digging into the edge of the table a little too roughly for a moment before easing back. "Not yet. What about the new interactive tourism app? I know you wanted to wait another month or two, but everyone else thinks it's ready. Deirdre has already spoken to Vance Eaton about it. They're interested and are excited about New Orleans being the debut city. We could sell it quickly, add a package for support and design tweaks to cover any bugs. Problem solved."

Alyssa tried not to let the ray of hope tempt her. The warmth of it was difficult to resist, but she didn't want to talk herself into one bad business decision simply to dodge another.

Mitch sat quietly, familiar with her need to work

through all the angles of a problem—or potential solution.

He was right. For the most part, the app was ready. The fine-tuning just required access to the specific requirements of the debut city. With its interactive, party atmosphere, New Orleans was exactly the kind of location she'd known would best utilize the application.

Tourist apps were a dime a dozen, but theirs married the best of social media with the latest information available. Constant updates would be provided, but as people communicated and interacted through the app there would be a continual stream of live information.

A great band was playing at a club? Someone could post pictures, videos and information. The line to get into an attraction was unusually long? People could post and help each other avoid unnecessary waits and wasted time. A group of college students were trying to connect in the crowd of Mardi Gras? Upload a photograph of your physical location.

It didn't escape her notice that both of the apps she'd focused on so far, at their core, were designed to bring people together. She didn't need a psych evaluation to figure out where that need grew from. At least something good could come from her lonely existence.

Focusing on one product launch at a time had seemed like the intelligent choice, especially since they'd never done one before, but now they no longer had that luxury.

With a nod, she agreed, "Make the call."

A sunny smile lit Mitch's eyes. "I already did."

Letting out a laugh, Alyssa punched Mitch in the arm. "Bastard. Then why did you even ask me?"

"I was laying groundwork we'd need eventually whether we pushed the timeline up or kept the release date a few months from now. You needed to come to the decision on your own."

"Right, with a not so subtle shove."

Mitch shrugged. "It's the right move."

For the first time in several days, the heavy weight crushing her chest eased away.

"I'll get the lawyers involved. Hopefully we'll have the details hammered out by Wednesday and a check in hand by close of business Friday."

Alyssa's gaze searched Mitch's deep chocolate eyes. She saw the same hope reflected back, which meant maybe she could actually let herself believe in it.

"You wanna tell me what that was all about?"

Alyssa knew instantly what he was talking about, but chose to pretend. "What do you mean?"

Mitch just cut her a glance that silently called *bullshit*. With a sigh, she gave in. "I have no idea."

And that scared the crap out of her. Whatever she'd expected when Beckett Kayne walked into her conference room, it wasn't the scorching awareness that had flared between them.

Or the interest she'd seen glowing out of those stormy blue eyes. Especially when, the last time he'd seen her, he'd dismissed her like the inexperienced child she'd been.

His parting words rang through her brain, sending a shudder down her spine.

No doubt Mitch saw it. A sound rolled up from his chest, a combination of concern and disbelief. "Be careful, Lys. Beckett Kayne isn't the kind of man who brings you candy and flowers. He's rough and unrelenting. He won't think twice about hurting you. Using you."

Mitch wasn't telling her anything her brain didn't already know. But her body… Apparently, it didn't give a flying flip.

Maybe to distract them both from that train of thought, Alyssa found herself blurting out words she hadn't meant to ever say. "I gave a random stranger a striptease last night."

That bombshell rocked Mitch backward. "Come again?"

Scrunching her nose, Alyssa sagged back into the welcome warmth of the leather chair. She stared at the pale blue wall opposite, better that than Mitch. He knew her too well and would immediately pick up on her conflicted response to the whole episode.

"Last night. I got home late. Had to walk through the crazy crowds."

"Expected."

Yeah, that's what she got living in the Quarter. A lot of residents lived close to Fat Tuesday, but she didn't have the time or money right now.

"I was so exhausted I didn't really think about it. I just started undressing, dreaming about collapsing into bed and dealing with the mess in the morning."

Mitch gave an empathetic grunt. He'd been working the same long hours and no doubt had collapsed bonelessly into his own bed last night.

"Something caught my attention. He moved maybe. I don't know. But I looked out my window to the balcony across the alley and saw a man standing there. He was almost completely in shadow, a mask obscuring half of his face."

Just the memory had her words going breathy. The way, even through the distance, his hot gaze had raked over her. The anticipation and tension. Need and excitement.

"I just…kept going."

"Jesus, Lys. What were you thinking? Don't you have enough problems right now? You really don't need to add a crazed stalker to the mix."

Mitch's words vaulted her out of the haze threatening to suck her back into the memory. Now was not the time. Not when her body was still on edge from her encounter with Kayne. That was a dangerous combination just begging for a spark to detonate.

"You're hilarious," she drawled out.

"I'm not being funny. I know you're oblivious to it, but you're gorgeous. Half of the single male population of New Orleans want inside your panties. And the other half just haven't met you yet."

It was easy for Alyssa to ignore his words. She could count on one hand the number of men she'd slept with and have a couple of fingers of left over for fun. She wasn't the kind of woman who got hit on in bars and never had been.

Mitch had to say stuff like that, though. It was the equivalent of most mothers saying their daughters were pretty.

"Seriously. And doing something that stupid during Mardi Gras…someone could have been taking pictures or taping you. You know people cross boundaries they'd never think about approaching any other time."

Mitch was right, but until last night she'd never been tempted to join the group of people who used Mardi Gras as an excuse to make bad behavior acceptable. She was far from a prude. Her motto tended more towards *c'est la vie* than *repent, you sinners*. It just wasn't her thing.

Until last night. It had been rather thrilling doing something so taboo.

That was the attraction. Really. That was all it was. She'd been upset and surrounded by happy drunks without a care in the world.

"I'll never see him again," she promised both Mitch and herself.

"Just…be careful."

"Aren't I always?"

Mitch grunted, a sound that could mean just about anything.

"If he shows up again you'll let me know? Let me make sure he isn't an escaped felon or alcoholic or—"

"A good guy, stealing a few moments of peace during a party held on the balcony of a multimillion-dollar home in the Quarter?"

"Just 'cause he got invited to a snooty party doesn't mean he's not dangerous."

"True."

As much as she wanted to reassure Mitch, there was something about her masked stranger that sent a delicious wave of foreboding prickling along her skin.

She was afraid the man watching her last night was very dangerous. And bold. And wickedly depraved.

The problem was that didn't bother Alyssa, although it definitely should.

BECKETT STARED OUT of the one-way window that looked over the twisting, gyrating mass of bodies below. Not even the double-paned glass could block the loud, thumping music blaring through the club.

Lights flashed, white, gold, green and blue, spinning, twirling and pulsing rhythmically.

Arms crossed over his chest, hips spread wide, he surveyed his domain. From his vantage point he could see the bar was three deep in people yelling for another round of drinks. He'd thought about scheduling another bartender, but with three working already it would have been a tight squeeze to get another person back there.

The customers didn't seem to mind the wait. Not when there was a line of people outside chomping at the bit to get in. Waitresses in deep-red bustiers, black satin boyshorts and silk thigh highs circulated through the room. Tonight, in a nod to Mardi Gras, they wore black feathered masks and had ropes of beads draped around their necks.

The three waiters working the floor all walked around naked from the waist up. That wasn't his requirement, but the guys quickly realized they made better tips that way. Besides, between the packed bodies and the heat generated from the dance floor, they all said it was cooler.

Beckett didn't care, as long as it didn't cause problems. Women were just as likely to have roaming hands as men, and sometimes when they drank they forgot their boyfriends were sitting there watching them fondle his staff.

Satisfied that everything was working smoothly tonight, Beckett's focus shifted from the floor to the walls and rafters. It was an old warehouse he'd converted, and there was plenty of room to handle the upgrades he wanted.

V&D's app was a twist on an interactive social media platform that dovetailed nicely with the theme of Exposed—sumptuous and gritty, in-your-face access.

Watch Me would connect to cameras set up to record and broadcast live feeds directly from each of his clubs. People anywhere could not only watch the party, but also interact.

He already had contractors ready to install huge

screens that would plaster the walls and ceiling. Several of them would project other locations—the New York feed would play on screens in Chicago. Someone from Iowa or Paris could hook up the feed and play it at their own makeshift party. And then upload videos of their experience, which would play over the screens in Seattle.

It essentially made the world one big, connected party.

To take it a step further, there was in-app communication. A guy in Geneva could message the beautiful girl in New Orleans he just watched dance and even send her a drink from the bar.

Global exposure and connection.

He could see it. Technology being used to bring people together instead of separating and isolating them.

What he couldn't understand was how Alyssa Vaughn didn't see the potential. Or didn't want to see it.

The memory of their meeting had conflicting emotions rolling through his body—frustration and urgency. His muscles tightened, his hands balled into fists.

The way her pale eyes had flashed at him, angry and full of disdain.

He'd thought of revealing who he was, but he didn't think she would have appreciated that revelation in company. And by the time the meeting was finished, he'd been so irritated and aroused he'd decided to keep the secret indefinitely.

He still had no idea what he'd done to her, but it was obvious her aversion to him went deeper than a simple business decision.

And he couldn't help but wonder how often she'd done something like that striptease last night. Was he a first? Or one in a long line of wanton experiences?

From out of nowhere, a surge of jealousy had his eyes

narrowing dangerously. That line of thinking would get him nowhere.

Needing the distraction, he slipped out of his office and through the cleverly concealed door in the wall, down onto the floor. He wasn't drunk or interested in dancing, but he had to weave through half the club to get to the bar.

On his way through, he lost count of how many times his ass was grabbed or palms slid across his chest. Someone even managed to slip fingers beneath the waistband of his jeans.

Clamping his hand around the offending wrist, he pulled the digits away from his skin. They were attached to a beautiful blonde, her body covered in a dark red dress that plunged in the front and stopped about four inches down her thighs. She smiled at him, blue eyes full of invitation.

Despite the way he used his grip on her arm to hold her away, her body undulated suggestively, as if she were plastered hard against him.

"Hi, sugar. Care to buy me a drink?" she asked, her lips smirking with promise.

It was impossible not to compare this woman to Alyssa. Blatant sexuality against bone-deep sensuality. This woman had everything she offered on display. There was no mystery. No challenge. He could have her upstairs across his desk in three minutes flat—only because it would take that long to get back to the office.

It had been a long time since Beckett had wanted easy.

Alyssa was all mystery, her wild streak hidden from prying eyes just as surely as the heavyhearted ink on her ribs. Everything about her was a question and contradiction.

If today had been their first meeting, he probably

would have walked away thinking she was innocently gorgeous, but positively untouchable. No doubt, he would still have been attracted to her, but he'd have figured she wasn't the kind of woman who could match him.

But last night…that changed everything. He'd seen beneath the perfect veneer. And he wanted more.

Maybe that's why he found himself turning around. And instead of heading to the bar to check on his employees, was out the door.

4

BECKETT LOUNGED ON the street, his eyes glued to the door of Alyssa's building. The press of people, swirl of madness and cacophony of sound surrounding him should have been distracting. But he couldn't tear his gaze from her door.

He shouldn't be here. Logically, he realized this was a bad idea. But, for some reason, his feet wouldn't obey the order to walk away.

Standing on the sidewalk outside her building was rather stupid, especially since he had no way of knowing if she was even home. Most people weren't. Not on a Saturday during Mardi Gras. The party raged right outside her front door and she was probably lost somewhere in the crowd, enjoying it.

While he was staked out here staring at her apartment like he might suddenly develop X-ray vision.

He'd wanted her last night when she'd given him a glimpse of herself. And he didn't just mean the smooth expanse of her skin. The fever of her desire. The way she'd reveled in his eyes on her. Her teasing and tempting. Bold and sensual. Daring.

It was the siren beneath her prim and proper exterior that held him captive. Instinct told him it was something she didn't share with many. He craved the moment she'd surrender and give in to the need snapping hot and dangerous between them.

Being pulled along by the frenzied atmosphere, Beckett had joined in, donning the same mask from the night before. A cup of beer clutched in his hand, he settled back against the wall. And forced his gaze to focus on the crowd instead of the apartment across the way.

He was mentally arguing with himself, trying to convince himself that he should leave, when she was suddenly there. Pausing just outside the door that protected her building from the madness, she stared into the throng, getting her bearings.

A small smile tugging her lips, she pushed through the crowd, heading for Canal and the Endymion parade that would roll through soon. She was too late to get close, people had been camped out for hours to save spots, but she didn't seem to care.

Unlike last night, she was no longer weighed down by exhaustion. An answering bubble of amusement rippled through his chest. He wanted to see her happy.

He wasn't sure why, but that realization surprised him.

Although that joviality didn't last for long. Not when, following her and debating whether or not to approach, he watched another man push into her personal space. The guy, most likely a college student—and from the looks of him an underage one, drunk off his ass—slammed into her.

Worry and anger twisted in Beckett's gut. Ignoring the glares and shouts, he started shoving at the wall of people blocking him from Alyssa. But he couldn't get to her fast enough.

His gaze never strayed, though. Huge clumsy hands wrapped around her hips, jerking her closer. Alyssa rocked back, going up onto the heels of the turquoise cowboy boots that hugged her calves. Who owned shoes that loud? He definitely wouldn't have expected it of the cool-and-collected Alyssa he'd faced off with across the table today.

Now the minx who'd teased him last night...those boots fit her perfectly, all wild and outlandish.

Drunk Frat Boy ran a hand up her naked arm, from wrist to shoulder. He squeezed, urging her against the wide expanse of his chest. Beckett had spent the past several years of his life watching men and women dance around each other, playing the attraction game. It was clear to him this guy wanted Alyssa. He wouldn't put it past the dude to have bumped into her on purpose.

Beckett's teeth ground together. His hands balled into fists and he shot forward ready to intervene.

But her reaction stopped him.

Tossing her head back, Alyssa laughed. The sight literally stopped him in his tracks. It...changed everything about her. Until that moment, he hadn't realized just how wistful her gaze had been. It was as if someone had flipped on a switch. It made his chest tighten and ache.

He'd seen the same pensive expression in his own mirror more times than he cared to remember.

Frozen, he watched her light green eyes sparkle. Her wide, luscious mouth stretched and opened. Instead of pulling away, she wrapped her long, elegant fingers around the guy's shoulders and went up on tiptoe as she leaned into him. Her mouth brushed close to his ear.

Beckett could see her lips moving, but there was no way to hear what she was saying above the din of music and noise.

Whatever it was, Beckett didn't like it. The guy's eyes, already glassy with too much alcohol, went completely glazed.

Alyssa patted Frat Boy's shoulder before slipping away. The guy stood there staring after her with the kind of expression that would make a devoted puppy envious. His friends snagged him and pulled him away, but his gaze stayed glued to Alyssa's retreating back until the mob swallowed him whole.

She wove in and out of the flood of humanity. Beckett couldn't look away. Unlike Frat Boy, he didn't have friends ready to pull him in the opposite direction. Somehow, he found himself behind her, watching the sway of her hips, as if the sight was water and he'd been crawling the desert for days.

A tight skirt—this one entirely different from last night's and this morning's—swished against the back of her thighs. The denim pockets were encrusted with a mess of rhinestones in matching fleur-de-lis. It hit a couple of inches above her knee, so wasn't indecent, especially compared to some of the other outfits on the street.

A filmy, almost see-through shirt the same color as her boots floated around her body, loose, breezy and falling off one shoulder. It bared a large expanse of her creamy skin. Beneath it, a black tank clung in all the right places.

Even casual, she managed to be sexy in an understated way that was more tempting than any blatant display of skin. He knew her secret, though. Beneath the facade she hid a wild little wanton.

Slipping into one of the bars, she grabbed a drink

and then came back outside to wander. Even when she reached the parade, she didn't really pay attention to it. Instead, she watched the people.

He paid attention to what drew her notice, collecting details she most likely wasn't aware of revealing. Watching for years from behind the barrier of his office window, he'd become rather adept at reading body language and people.

A family. A mom and dad with their arms draped around each other. Two kids, a boy and a girl, both teens, shoving at each other, bickering and bantering. Until someone knocked into the girl, and the boy went immediately into protective mode, pushing her behind the wall of his gangly, developing body. The parents exchanged an indulgent glance.

Alyssa let out a deep sigh, her expression making him curious. A half smile tugged at her lips, but her eyes were full of disappointment, longing and hurt.

He didn't like that at all.

There were plenty of men on the streets. Beckett watched quite a few of them turn to stare as Alyssa passed by. But she was completely oblivious to the scrutiny. And not once did her gaze sweep across any of them with interest.

However, she noticed the couples. Their heads bent close. A guy whispering in his lover's ear. A couple with their hands lodged in each other's back pockets. She took it all in, ambling along as though she had nowhere to be and nothing more weighty on her mind than what her next drink would be.

Finally, she turned a corner to a side street that was a little less crowded. About halfway down the block she stopped. Around her, people streamed by, but she didn't notice. Her gaze was riveted to something in the shadows of a deep alcove between two buildings.

Chancing discovery, Beckett moved closer until he could see what had caught her attention.

Something dark and hot surged through his blood when he realized she was staring at a couple blatantly making out. They weren't trying to cover up what they were doing. Actually, they gave every impression of being completely oblivious that anyone else in the world existed.

The pale expanse of a leg wrapped tight around a denim-clad male hip shone in the light from the streetlamps. The man's hands were pressed against the wall on either side of the woman's head, but his entire body touched her from lips to chest to hip. Her fingers gripped his hair, holding him tight to her mouth.

They were devouring each other and, if they didn't pull away, would eventually be giving anyone walking by a free show.

Beckett took all this in with a three-second glance. He couldn't have cared less about the couple. What held him entranced was Alyssa's response to them.

She was turned on. More than that. Her chest rose and fell on quick, shallow breaths.

Her mouth was open, but he watched her tongue sneak out, sweeping across the deep pink of her bottom lip, leaving it wet and glistening. He wanted to taste her lips and find out just how sweet they'd be.

Moving quickly, Beckett closed the space between them. His chest collided with her back and his hands settled gently on her hips, holding her still. Her body jolted.

Slipping one arm around her waist, Beckett let his other slide up her ribs. Cupping her cheek in his palm, he coaxed her to turn to him. To see him. Her frantic gaze darted across his masked face. Recognition shot through her and her tensed body immediately softened.

She stilled and then melted into him. Beckett accepted her weight and the spreading warmth of finally having her loose and lax in his arms.

Her pupils dilated, not with anxiety or fear, but barely suppressed excitement.

That realization only stoked his already chaotic emotions higher.

"What are you doing here?" she breathed.

"Did you really think I'd let you get away with shutting me out?" he asked. "Tell me to let you go. Or get lost. But let me taste you first. Once. Please," he begged, right before finally claiming her mouth.

GOD, SHE WAS kissing a complete stranger in the middle of Mardi Gras. No, that wasn't true. She might be participating, but there was no mistaking just who was controlling this moment.

And it wasn't her.

She was simply along for the ride. Swept away on the current of sensation. His hard fingers, cupping her jaw, held her still. The band of his arm across her belly pulled her close, as if letting her go would devastate him. His warmth radiated through her and seeped deep into her bones.

The unmistakable ridge of masculine arousal nestled tight against the small of her back. Alyssa's hips rolled against him. An unconscious movement, but it felt good knowing she had that effect on him.

Because he had the same effect on her.

Maybe that's why she went with the moment and didn't

fight him or herself. In the middle of a public street, he completely consumed her. And, unlike the couple in the shadows, he made no attempt to hide.

Despite everything, this was safe. At least a hell of a lot safer than the frantic, unwanted thoughts of Beckett Kayne she'd been fighting all night. This kiss, these moments, made her forget everything except the masked man holding her. The way he made her body respond and her brain simply shut down leaving nothing but…pure sensation and unfiltered response.

Maybe it was her imagination that added the slide of multiple gazes across her body, across them. She wanted them to watch. Wanted someone else to see what was happening to her.

To make it real.

The feathers from his mask tickled her skin. His mouth, somehow both hard and soft, moved against hers, demanding and restrained. He knew exactly what he was doing and methodically enthralled her.

His tongue thrust between her lips, taking whatever he wanted from her. It was sweet and sharp. Heaven and absolute hell, because in the same moment he'd surprised her he'd also managed to pin her arms uselessly to her sides.

She struggled against him, not to get free, but so she could participate, do something more than surrender and melt.

With a gasp that burst across her open, wet lips, he tore his mouth free. But didn't let go. Instead, he used his hold to turn her head and expose the long column of her throat.

A trail of fire followed his lips. A shiver jolted down her spine and raised the tiny hairs on the back of her neck.

He chuckled, dragging his mouth across the evidence of her instinctive reaction. The sound of it, deep, warm and entirely egotistical, resonated through her body, settling deep between her thighs with a pressing ache.

How could his pleased response ratchet up her own desire? She didn't need or want his approval. Had given up the need for that kind of validation from anyone a long time ago.

She didn't even know his name!

"Who are you?" she breathed out on a ragged sigh when his teeth scraped down the straining tendon in her throat.

He'd come up behind her so swiftly. All she could see of him now was the bulging weight of his biceps as he held her in place. Before, she'd gotten the briefest glimpse of his hot, glittering eyes. His face was obscured by that damn mask. And his mouth…sensual, luscious lips.

She couldn't see him, so instead filled her other senses with whatever clues she could take in.

Stopping her struggle to free her arms, she turned her palms and grasped hard thighs. Her fingers dug into heavy muscles. Denim scraped across her sensitive fingertips. It was worn and soft, the heat of him seeping through the thinning threads.

The night before he'd been dressed more formally. Dark slacks, a dress shirt unbuttoned at his throat and the cuffs rolled up his strong arms. She'd assumed he was a businessman who'd come straight from the office to whatever party raged across the alley.

She knew her neighbor worked at a law firm, perhaps he was a lawyer, as well? He was strong enough, forceful enough to be formidable in a courtroom. Part of her could see him, arguing passionately in front of a group of rapt people.

But there was something about the vision that didn't fit. He…had a primal edge that couldn't be tamed by convention and laws.

The shirt scraping her cheek was soft cotton, a gray so dark it bordered on black, and for some reason it reminded her of the brief flash of his eyes. Since they were hidden by the mask, she couldn't tell their exact color, although the gleam of desire had been more than clear.

Because it was all she could do, Alyssa used the inch of space he'd given her to rub against him, his chest unbelievably solid beneath her cheek.

"I'm not going to tell you." Grazing his lips against the sensitive shell of her ear, he whispered, "You like not knowing who I am. Admit it. It makes you feel daring and wicked and more than a little turned on to have a stranger touching you in the middle of a public street."

The tip of his tongue flicked out, leaving a throbbing trail across the skin behind her ear. He paused long enough to suck. Her body sagged against him, turned on more by his words than his touch.

He was right.

"I watched you. Watched you watching them."

Slowly, he turned her head until her eyes were directed back to the shadows and the couple still hidden there. In the time she'd been distracted they'd gone further.

The guy's hands were no longer pressed against the brick. One hand now encircled both of the woman's wrists, holding them prisoner high above her head. His other hand slid across her body. Her shirt bunched up just beneath the swell of her breasts, exposing the curve of her ribs and belly. His hand disappeared, covering the swell of her breast. Her head dropped back against the wall, mouth falling open in ecstasy.

Alyssa felt the caress as if it had been to her own body. Her nipples tingled and tightened painfully. She ached. And arched her back to thrust her own breasts up in silent supplication. She wanted him to touch. To ease the thumping need.

But he didn't.

Instead he said, "Do you know how beautiful you are? Sensual and gorgeous. Your skin flushed pink. Your eyes glazed. I can feel the current running beneath your skin, anticipation and lust. If I trailed my fingers up beneath the hem of your skirt I'd find you so hot and wet."

Her breath hitched in her lungs. Her fingers dug harder into his thighs. He was right. Her panties were soaked, the slick glide of them against her skin a new brand of torture.

And he'd barely touched her. Certainly not where it counted most.

She didn't mean to do it. Wasn't even aware she wanted to until the single word fell from her parted lips. But she begged. "Please."

His lips trailed across her jaw. "Please what?"

"Touch me."

"Now? Here? Where anyone and everyone could see?"

Swallowing hard, Alyssa nodded her head. She didn't care. Was far beyond that point. Everyone acted crazy during Mardi Gras, she rationalized. Really, it was so simple. If he didn't touch in her in the next few seconds she was afraid she might die. Expire from frustration and desire.

A tortured growl rumbled through his chest. The echo of it vibrated across her own skin.

When he slid his hand over her belly, Alyssa fought to contain the whimper of relief that threatened to break free. Down her hip. Along her thigh. His fingertips grazed the expanse of skin beneath the hem of her skirt.

She was free of his hold, but now she stood frozen of her own accord, afraid if she moved a single inch he'd stop the beautiful torture. Cupping her face, he guided her back to him, claiming her mouth.

Pouring every ounce of longing into the connection, she met his kiss and matched him. She wasn't content to simply acquiesce, but demanded a piece of him for herself. Her teeth scraped across his bottom lip. Her tongue darted in to get a better taste.

The whole time his fingers slid higher and higher up the inside of her thigh. Her skirt bunched at his wrist, quickly approaching the level of indecent. But she was too far gone to care.

Until he stopped—his hand, his mouth. And pulled back.

Disoriented, Alyssa blinked up into his hidden gaze.

His teeth closed delicately around her earlobe. She felt the gentle tug deep at her throbbing core.

"Last night I went home hard and frustrated that you'd teased me, turned me on and then shut me out. Tonight it's my turn to walk away."

Alyssa drew in a sharp breath, ready to protest. But her brain was too busy spinning on his revelation. Last night he'd been as turned on as she had. Just as frustrated and unfulfilled. He'd felt the connection, even through the distance between them.

It hadn't just been a figment of her tired, deprived, overactive imagination.

"Unlike last night, I won't torture you with the possibility we might never finish what we started. Let me assure you, we will."

Her body quaked, thrills and trepidation twining together.

His hold on her tightened. "I want to bury myself in your body. Watch the expression on your face as you let go and give in to the euphoria building between us. You will be mine, Alyssa Vaughn."

And then he was gone. Just…gone. Her burning body was suddenly cold and achingly alone.

She was so tired of being alone.

Spinning around, Alyssa's eyes searched through the crowd, desperate for at least one glimpse. But he didn't even leave her that.

What he did give her was the realization that he knew her name. And she wasn't entirely certain how to feel about that.

It should probably scare her. Obviously, he'd had a productive day if in less than twenty-four hours he'd figured out who she was. This guy could be anyone, and the fact that he'd taken the time to research her should have had warning bells clanging through her brain.

Her highly tuned self-preservation instincts were surprisingly silent.

However, the entirely girly thrill wasn't.

He'd taken the time to find out who she was. He wanted her.

JESUS, HE'D ALMOST gone too far.

He'd been so wrapped up in the sensation and scent of her he'd forgotten where they were.

Scraping a hand through his hair, Beckett silently berated himself.

Alyssa might get off on watching and being watched, but that hardly gave him the right to push her to a mindless frenzy in the middle of a crowded street and toward something she'd most likely regret the moment it was over.

And he'd be damned if she'd regret a single thing they did together.

Especially after experiencing the unbridled way she'd put herself completely in his hands. They might be adversaries in the boardroom, but she completely trusted him with her body. Even if she wasn't aware that's what she was doing.

And he wouldn't abuse that gift.

Another growl of frustration rumbled through his chest. Beckett blended into the crowd, pulling off the mask and changing his posture. He slumped, shoulders rounding and head dropping down. Even though it looked as if he studied the pavement, his gaze never shifted from Alyssa.

He was going to make sure she got home safely. He, more than most, realized the kind of bad things that could happen late at night. And that was before adding the craziness and lack of restraint that accompanied Mardi Gras.

Shoving his hands deep into his pockets, he followed her. Her gait was no longer mindless and ambling. She walked with purpose, her strides eating up ground and taking her home at a fast clip.

When he'd come out tonight, loitering across from her apartment, there'd really only been one thought on his mind—possessing her.

And while he still wanted that, something about the encounter they'd just shared changed everything.

Before, he hadn't been thinking about her, not really. He'd let the buzz of their sparring match this morning and the residual frustration from the night before cloud his thinking.

And he didn't like what that realization said about him. Not at all.

Tonight she'd given him something unexpected—her vulnerability.

It was another side of her, something softer that made him want to protect and please her. Not the teasing minx or the sharp, determined businesswoman. In both of their previous encounters she'd exuded a harsh confidence that pinged every instinct he had. He'd never been one to walk away from a challenge.

But tonight he'd realized it had all been a bluff. Or, mostly a bluff, hiding a deep vulnerability that made him want to protect her.

He had no doubt she would continue to challenge him and he wanted that, desperately. Arguing with her this morning had gotten his blood flowing in a way he hadn't experienced in a long time.

Alyssa slipped behind the fence surrounding her building.

While he'd obviously decided to play this straight, that didn't mean he wasn't opposed to stacking the deck in his favor. He was fair, not stupid.

He'd vowed to protect her and he was going to fulfill that promise, providing the perfect opportunity for her to explore the desires she kept locked down in a safe environment.

A smile of anticipation curled Beckett's lips. If she

wasn't already hooked, there was no way she'd be able to walk away from what he planned next.

Not even when she discovered the mystery man who could make her body burn was the same one she wanted to hate.

5

It HAD BEEN two days since Alyssa had seen or heard from her masked stranger. And her body had been humming the entire time, a kind of deep-seated arousal nothing could cure. It left her fidgety and restless. Nothing, not even work, managed to settle her.

She didn't like feeling this way. Out of control. Reactive. It reminded her of walking on eggshells around her father and stepmother. Tension tightening her shoulders because she had no idea when the next verbal punch would come.

Everything reminded her of him. The slide of her shirt against her stomach. A puff of air across her neck. The scent of coffee and mint.

God, this was the last thing she needed right now. Her focus should have been squarely on Kayne and how she was going to prevent him from taking everything from her. Instead, she couldn't concentrate. Not the best frame of mind for negotiations.

Taking a deep breath, Alyssa had forced her brain to focus. In less than twenty minutes she and Mitch would be sitting down with Vance Eaton, who expected a preview of her tourism app.

This was too important to screw up. It was their lifeline, and she needed her head in the game.

Two hours later, Alyssa was biting back the elation that wanted to escape. They'd won. For the first time since Mitch told her the loan was being called due early she could take a full breath. The weight that had been holding her down had disappeared. Until that moment she hadn't realized just how desperately afraid she'd been.

But, if they could work out the small details, she was almost certain Vance Eaton would buy the app. Problems solved. Disaster averted. Beckett Kayne thwarted.

She had to admit, *that* more than anything was responsible for the goofy grin permanently affixed to her face. On her way out the door Megan, their receptionist, asked her to come out for a little Mardi Gras fun. Normally, Alyssa would have declined, but for some reason she found herself saying yes.

Excitement flashing in her bright blue eyes, Megan had clapped her hands and squealed. "I'll pick you up around eight."

Alyssa had just nodded her head, deciding to sit back and enjoy the ride. Megan was always trying to get her out. The party scene had never been her thing, but she wanted to be seen tonight.

A chill of anticipation tripped down her spine. Maybe if she was out her masked stranger would resurface. He'd promised they weren't done.

So she'd come home from the office and spent the past two hours getting ready. Fussing with her makeup and second-guessing her outfit. Alyssa couldn't remember the last time she'd cared. And it was all her masked stranger's fault. The prospect, no matter how slim, of seeing him had her tied in knots.

Alyssa Vaughn didn't get tied in knots over men. Ever. Until now.

Her buzzer sounded and Megan's crystal-bell voice floated out to her through the speaker. "Get your ass out here, girlie. I'm ready to party!"

Shaking her head, Alyssa grabbed her clutch and her silver pashmina, wrapping it tight around her shoulders. It kept her from feeling almost naked in the short leather miniskirt and tight sequined top she'd put on. They were outside her normal comfort zone but, knowing Megan, appropriate for whatever her friend had in mind.

Tonight she was going to live a little. Like everyone else in New Orleans.

They had to fight through the Monday evening crowd to get to the car Megan had left blocks away. Parking was a bitch, but they were both too excited to get annoyed.

Alyssa was riding the wave of anticipation and didn't realize just where they were going until it was too late.

When they parked outside the huge structure, Alyssa looked up at the innocuous facade of Exposed—the last place she wanted to visit. Just the appearance of the industrial building with the line of antsy people waiting outside was enough to deflate her bubble of enthusiasm.

She looked at Megan, with her cropped white-blond hair, pixie face and tiny stature, and contemplated leaving before their night had even begun.

"Why are we here?"

The wicked grin Megan flashed her did nothing to soothe Alyssa's nerves. "Keep your friends close and enemies closer. If nothing else, you can gather intel on

Kayne. Besides, my roommate's boyfriend is a bartender here. He put us on the VIP list."

She couldn't leave. Not unless she wanted Megan giving her hell for being a coward. A drink, maybe two, and she could plead exhaustion and head home.

Taking a deep breath, Alyssa forced her feet to move. The bouncer consulted a list and waved them past grumbles from those still waiting in line. She tried not to let her lips curl with distaste when she walked through the door.

There was nothing physically wrong with Exposed. Alyssa's issues were focused squarely on the owner himself. God, she hoped he wasn't here tonight. The last thing she needed was to run into the man. At least in the boardroom she had a chance of remembering the contention between them instead of the awareness. In the middle of a dark, crowded club...

Megan wouldn't let her linger by the door and shoved her along with the sheer force of her enthusiasm. They were both pressed tight to the bar ordering drinks from the guy Megan knew in no time. The crush of humanity here was almost as bad as the throng they'd left behind on Canal Street.

The benefit was Alyssa's ability to hide behind the shield of people. The music, something with a heavy techno beat, settled deep inside her chest, making her muscles twitch and pulse.

It was obvious Beckett Kayne was making plenty of money. Although she'd already known that. Twelve locations in some of the most expensive cities across the country. The man was doing just fine.

For some reason, that only made her more uptight.

Her eyes darted over the crowd, as if he might rise out of it like a serpent from the sea.

Two drinks and forty-five minutes later, Alyssa finally started to relax. Megan had been back and forth to the dance floor multiple times. But once she'd found a seat, Alyssa hadn't moved from it, despite being asked several times if she wanted to dance.

"Come on, stick-in-the-mud, come out there with me," Megan whined, tugging on Alyssa's arm. Maybe it was the alcohol, or Megan's stubborn insistence, but she finally gave in.

That's how she found herself in the middle of a pack of sweaty, drunk and gorgeous people. Megan fit in perfectly, apparently having already made friends. She laughed and leaned close to hear what one of the guys yelled into her ear.

Alyssa rolled her hips, her body responding instinctively to the deep-throated beat of the music blaring around them. Laser lights flashed, the pulse adding to the throb building inside her.

Hands slipped around her hips, pulling her back against a hard body. For the briefest second, Alyssa's cloudy brain thought it was her stranger, but even before she glanced back she knew it wasn't.

While the masculine wall of flesh at her back was nice enough, she didn't respond on an instinctive level.

But combined with the buzz of alcohol, she wasn't going to ignore the pleasant way the man's interest made her feel. Being wanted was a seduction all its own. And by the way the man looked at her, his eyes running appreciatively over her body, she knew he wanted her. Knowing it was nothing more than a harmless flirtation, Alyssa gave in to the moment. She let her body follow his lead, gyrating, swirling and grinding.

Her eyes closed, her imagination conjuring up other hands and hips. Until suddenly the warm wall of masculinity at her back was replaced by a breeze. The shock, more than anything, had Alyssa twisting around to figure out what had happened.

Air seized in her lungs when she realized.

Beckett Kayne had his hand wrapped around the back of the guy's neck. He wasn't doing anything wrong, exactly, simply holding the guy, but it was clear from the expression on Beckett's face that he was pissed.

Leaning in, Beckett whispered something close to his captive's face. The guy's eyes went wide, sliding to her before jerking back to Beckett's. The guy nodded, a single, quick movement, which was all he could manage beneath Beckett's tight grasp.

His mouth twisting into a grimace, Beckett released the man, but let his hand hover in the air as if waiting for the guy to make one wrong move.

Alyssa couldn't breathe. She stood stock still, waiting, her body humming with concern, conflict and feminine appreciation. She hated herself a little for that last one.

But she wasn't blind. Every woman in the place had her eyes trained on Beckett Kayne. His chest and arm muscles strained against the confines of his black T-shirt, which looked as if it might give up the fight and rip at any moment. The jeans practically poured around his lower body didn't help, either.

God, he was hot. And her brain telling her that physical perfection wasn't everything didn't seem to help.

Not even considering he'd just stuck his nose where it didn't belong.

That thought finally shook her out of her stupor.

Closing the gap between them, she pressed into Beckett's personal space. "What do you think you're doing?"

"Saving you from making a stupid mistake."

"I was dancing with a guy at a club, not taking him into the alley for a quick grope."

A low sound rumbled through Beckett's chest. An ominous warning flashed in his blue-gray eyes. Stepping closer, he crowded into her personal space. What was wrong with her that she wanted—hoped—he would put his hands on her hips just as the guy he'd scared off had?

She shouldn't want that. She *didn't* want that. Not really.

Disappointment was not swelling through her when, instead of bringing their bodies flush, Beckett grasped her hand and turned away.

The crowd parted like the Red Sea, making a clear path for him. She'd had to push and shove to get anywhere. It bugged the heck out of her, the ease with which everything came to him.

He was the perfect example of the silver-spoon set, having everything handed to him on a platter. Even when it had been taken from him, he'd managed to land on his feet…rather quickly.

Dragging her behind him, Beckett opened a door in the wall she hadn't even realized was there. Behind it were a darkened hallway and stairs leading up to an office. The moment they were both inside, he dropped her hand. She didn't appreciate the way her skin prickled, as if the loss of his touch was painful.

Shaking her hand to try and rid herself of the reaction, Alyssa crossed her arms and tucked her hands close to her body. Her gaze landed on the floor-to-ceiling wall of glass that looked out over the expanse of the club below.

"I had no idea this was up here," she said, wandering closer for a better look. "You can't see it from down there."

"Good," Beckett grunted.

Slipping up beside her, he mirrored her body language. "What are you doing here, Alyssa?"

"I came to a club with a friend. One who's probably wondering where I went."

Alyssa felt the impact when he twisted his gaze away from the crowd and directed it at her. Here they were isolated, even the pounding sound of music muffled behind the thick glass.

"I already had security let her know you're up here with me."

When on earth had he done that? Certainly not since he approached her on the dance floor. A sudden thought blasted through her brain. Without letting it filter through, Alyssa blurted out, "Were you watching me?"

"Yes." No explanation, justification or apology, just blatant honesty.

The gravity of that single word pressed against her. She felt suspended, and not just because they were high above the people churning below like class-five rapids. Something was happening, and Alyssa wasn't entirely certain she wanted it to.

"Why?"

"Let's just say Exposed is the last place I expected to see you."

For some reason that bothered her. "Why? Because I don't fit in?"

A frown marred Beckett's beautiful face. "No, because you've made it clear what you think about me."

It was her turn to look surprised. "Oh? What do I think of you?"

"Obviously, not much."

Alyssa scoffed. "I find it hard to believe the man who stands behind a wall of glass surveying his domain like a feudal lord needs me to stroke his ego."

Out of nowhere the atmosphere shifted. Something hot and alarmingly loaded crackled between them. Alyssa could practically smell burnt ozone and passion.

Leaning close, Beckett brought them nose to nose. He stared deep into her eyes. "My ego isn't what I want you to stroke."

A sharp breath whistled through her teeth. Beneath his words and intense stare, she was frozen. Her throat was dry and her mouth refused to work. Words screamed through her head, but she couldn't force them out.

Her body hummed, energy and anticipation flowing just beneath her skin.

No, this wasn't what she wanted. Or needed.

Forcing her tongue across suddenly numb lips, she whispered, "Too bad. Not gonna happen."

He smiled, a wolfish twist of his lips that did nothing to cool the need flaring deep inside her.

As if realizing he was pushing her too far, Beckett stepped back. With him out of her personal space, she could finally breathe again. Her lungs pulled in a huge gulp of air.

She should leave. But she didn't. Instead, she stood there, watching the push and pull of people below. She spotted Megan in the throng, caught between two men who seemed perfectly willing to share her attention.

After several minutes, Alyssa's shoulders began to relax again.

"Can you see it?" Beckett finally asked.

"See what?"

Canting his head sideways, he drilled her with that blue-gray gaze. "The screens. The cameras. The app and interaction filling this place."

He pointed to the exposed rafters, his words painting pictures she didn't want to see, but could.

She could see what he was talking about because, as much as she hadn't wanted to, she'd read his proposal. And his vision worked perfectly with what she'd imagined for the app.

She'd wanted something that would break down barriers and bring people together.

If anyone else had presented her with Beckett's proposal she would have leaped at the chance to work together.

But she refused to let him know that.

"No," she said, her voice harsh. "I can't see it."

Alyssa stormed away, her sharp words ripping through him. Why did it bother him so much? It had been a long time since he'd let anyone's opinion of him matter. What hold did this woman have over him that she meant something?

He should let her go. And he tried. But he couldn't concentrate. Not when she was down there, dancing, drinking and flirting with random strangers.

The memory of her stripping for him kept tormenting him, interspersed with the vision of that goon's hands on her hips and his body plastered against her. Beckett didn't want her taking her clothes off for anyone else.

Finally, he gave up any pretense of working and stalked back to the window.

She was easy to spot—apparently he had a sixth sense where Alyssa Vaughn was concerned.

Her friend was sandwiched between two guys, and since they were at least a foot taller she almost disappeared. But that flash of platinum blond was hard to miss. The men had their hands all over her body, and the little pixie didn't seem to mind at all.

Beckett had seen enough hookups to recognize a wild night in the making.

Several feet away, Alyssa was oblivious to the male attention centered squarely on her pulsing body. She held a drink in her hand, something pink and girlie. Even from this distance it was clear she'd managed to down a few more of them since she'd walked out of his office.

The night she'd danced solely for him she'd been graceful and fluid, but now her body was made of liquid silver—rolling, gyrating, pumping. Her eyes were closed, the music flowing straight through her muscles.

Around her, a tiny circle of spectators had formed. Several of the men reached out, running their hands over her to try and coax her toward them. But the moment someone touched, Alyssa twisted away. It was clear she wasn't interested.

He should stay upstairs. He knew it. But after fifteen minutes of watching, every muscle in his body was pulled so tight he was afraid they would all snap.

And it was a damn good thing he was paying attention or he might have missed it.

Standing at his window, he watched Alyssa push against the throng at the bar and order another drink.

The minute the bartender placed it in front of her, a guy to her left leaned in close and yelled something to her.

Turning, she answered. And while she wasn't looking the guy to her right slipped something into her drink.

"Goddammit," Beckett snarled beneath his breath.

Snatching up the radio connected to the com units all of his security staff wore, he was barking orders at his head of security before he was halfway across his office. "We've got a guy spiking drinks. By the bar. Late twenties, blond hair, wearing a red T-shirt. Get him and his friend."

Heart pounding, he raced onto the dance floor, pushing and shoving his way through the crowd. Why the hell didn't his bartenders have coms? He was fixing that first thing tomorrow. He should have had a way to communicate with them, have them pull Alyssa's drink before she could swallow any.

By the time he reached her, he knew it was too late. Her glass was half empty. Security had reached them first, although Alyssa obviously had no idea what was going on. Beckett's priority had been detaining the guys so he could figure out what she'd been given.

Two burly guys had collared the assholes. Wrapping their arms behind their bodies and holding them with beefy hands at their necks, the two were already being led toward the back of the club. They were struggling, yelling and protesting. But no one was stopping to help. In fact, the crowd around simply scooted out of the way, gawking at the show.

He paid good money for intimidating security who knew what they were doing. Not many people were willing to mess with them, especially when they didn't have a dog in the fight.

Wrapping an arm around Alyssa's waist, Beckett swept her along in the wake of the four men.

"What are you doing?" she asked, fighting his hold.

"Saving your ass."

She tried to twist away. "From what? The only thing I need saving from is *you*."

He had to give it to her, she was lithe and fast. The little minx slipped right through his fingers, twisting back around to the bar and the drink she'd left there. She had it halfway to her lips already when he reached her again.

He smacked it straight out of her hand. The cup clattered back to the bar, the rest of the contents spilling across the surface. His bartender, who'd clued in to what must be going on, was already there waiting for instructions.

"Clean this up," Beckett ordered right over Alyssa's "What the hell?"

She shoved him. But Beckett was past the point of soft and easy. Someone had tried to hurt her. Most likely planned to rape her. And she was fighting him.

Cornering her against the bar, he leaned in real close. Staring straight into her wide, pale eyes, he growled, "Those two assholes spiked your drink. Would you please stop fighting me so I can figure out what they gave you and take care of you?"

Alyssa's mouth popped open. Her dark pink lips were an unintentional invitation he was having a very hard time ignoring, but kissing her right now was a bad idea. Very bad.

A strangled squeak finally escaped and he watched her entire body sag against the hard edge of the bar. Wrapping his arm around her waist again, he tugged her back into the shelter of his body.

This time she didn't protest, but went quietly, allowing him to clear a path through the crowd for them both.

They were back in the darkened, quiet hallway again when the radio on his hip squawked. "GHB, boss."

Beckett swore.

"What does that mean?" Alyssa asked in a small voice that made his chest ache and his fists clench with the need to punch something. Hard.

Hitting the button, he ordered, "Call the cops. Have the incident reported. I doubt this is their first rodeo. And then ban them from every single one of my goddamn clubs for life."

God, he hated predators. Especially the ones who thought they could come into his house and use it like their personal playground.

There'd been a time in his life when he would have taken care of the problem personally. But as much as his instincts were screaming at him to pound them into the ground for trying to hurt Alyssa, he couldn't do that.

"You wanna talk to them first, boss?"

He was smart enough to realize if he came within ten feet of them his control was likely to snap.

"No," he ground out. Besides, Alyssa was his first priority. GHB was fairly fast acting. She was probably going to start feeling the effects at any moment. "Tell the cops I have the victim and she'll come in tomorrow to make her statement. I have my cell if you need me. Understand?"

"Loud and clear."

Beckett didn't slow until they were in the lot behind the club where his employees parked. It was safer to keep them separated from patrons. That way he and his security staff could control access.

His low, sleek Maserati sat right by the door, black

as night. He loved his car. It was one of the first things he'd bought for himself when he'd become successful. It wasn't the latest and greatest, which his father delighted in pointing out every chance he got. But that wasn't because he couldn't afford something newer and flashier.

This car was his. He'd earned it on his own. And he was damn proud of that.

Opening the passenger door, Beckett ushered Alyssa in. She hesitated for several seconds but finally sat without protest. He was grateful for small miracles.

Rounding the hood, he was inside and shooting through the parking lot as soon as she'd had a chance to snap on her seat belt.

"Text your friend. Let her know what happened and that you're safe."

"I don't know what happened," she said, but pulled out her cell anyway.

"You've been given GHB. Liquid Ecstasy."

She made a small sound.

"Turn the car around."

Beckett glanced at her. She sat there, her body enveloped by the protective leather of his car. Pissed. Her body vibrated with barely controlled fury, skin flushed hot and eyes burning.

"Why?"

"So I can kill them," she growled.

Beckett couldn't stop the laughter, not at the mental image of her taking her pound of flesh from both of the guys—he had no doubt she could pull it off. She might be small, but she was strong and probably packed a hell of a punch.

Part of him wanted to do what she'd asked. She deserved the chance, if nothing else. Besides, that was a sight he'd surely love to see, her face flushed with anger, those green eyes flashing with determination and danger.

The problem was that in a few minutes she wasn't going to be in any physical shape to follow through on the bloodlust coloring her features.

"Not gonna happen, princess."

Transferring her anger to the easy target, Alyssa's charged gaze swung to him. He could feel the fiery slice of it running across him, but kept his eyes trained on the road.

"Where are you taking me?"

"To my place."

"No. Take me home."

Beckett just shook his head. "It's Mardi Gras, Alyssa. You live in the Quarter. Any minute now the drug is going to kick in and you're not going to be in any shape to fight your way through that to get home."

"I'll be fine," she ground out between clenched teeth.

"Ever taken GHB?"

"No."

Beckett shot her a pointed look. "You're going to get touchy-feely and euphoric. Sexually stimulated. You want to be alone when that happens?"

"Better than with you. I don't trust you."

He shrugged. "You don't have to. I don't take advantage of intoxicated women."

Something dark and dangerous flashed across her features. Her mouth thinned into a tight line. She was angry. With him. But he had no idea why.

And he really didn't have time to figure it out. At least, not now.

"I've already called a friend, a neighbor who works as a doctor in the emergency room. She'll come over and check you out, draw blood. The police will want a drug test so they can charge the guys responsible."

Beckett pulled into the underground garage beneath his apartment complex. Without waiting for further protest, he jumped from the car and stalked around the hood.

Before he could get to her, the door was flung open. Alyssa leaped out, her feet spread wide and her hands balled into fists on her hips. She glared at him, her chest rising and falling as if she'd just run several miles. He tried not to notice the swell of her breasts pressing against the liquid silver of her top, but it was damn hard.

Her mouth opened. He had no doubt that whatever she was about to say was only going to piss him off. But before any words could fall, the strangest expression crossed her face. And then she swayed.

"Damn," Beckett swore under his breath, surging forward to grab her.

Alyssa's body slumped against his car. She stared up at him with those pale-green eyes that had the ability to cut straight through him. They were wide and unfocused, her pupils dilated.

Reaching up, he smoothed the stray strands of hair that had fallen out of her high ponytail.

Her mouth snapped shut. A soft whimper slipped out as she pushed her cheek into his fingers. She turned for more, searching for the stimulation and pleasure of touch.

He tried to tell himself any touch would be getting this reaction from her right now. She was high. But as she tried to nuzzle closer, his body didn't understand the distinction.

Dropping his hand from her skin was one of the hardest things he'd ever had to do. Putting space between them, he bent down. Staring her in the eye he said,

"You're safe with me, Alyssa. I promise. This happened at *my* club. Let me take care of you."

Slowly, she nodded and tried to take a step away from his car. She stumbled. Without pause, Beckett swept her up into his arms.

Her hands dropped around his neck, burying deep in the hair at his nape and holding tight. Her face snuggled into his throat. She sighed, the gust of air tickling his skin and making him throb and ache.

A few minutes of torture and he could have her safely in his guest bedroom.

Her hot lips found his skin. Beckett bit back a groan. She trailed her mouth down his neck and shoulder, kissing, nipping and driving him insane.

With insistent fingers, she tugged at his shirt collar, trying to get access to more. Every cell in his body was begging him to stop moving and give her exactly what she wanted. What they both wanted.

But he'd regret that. And so would she—if she remembered. He didn't want that.

The first time he had her, Beckett wanted her to remember every earthshaking moment.

Trying to disengage her hold on his clothes without dropping her was like fighting an octopus. The woman was stronger than she looked. Especially when she wanted something.

Which only stoked the fire in his gut higher.

He'd already known she'd be wild in bed when she finally let free.

Clenching his teeth, Beckett fought every instinct screaming inside his head. He'd never been so happy to make it into his penthouse. Alyssa didn't even pause to look around, just kept touching and kissing and teasing.

"God, you feel so good. Soft and silky and…hmmm," she purred in the back of her throat, brushing her lips back and forth across his skin.

"Men don't appreciate being called soft, princess," Beckett admonished.

"But you are." Her words were slurred. "Sleek and soft on top, but underneath…all compact, hard muscle. What the hell do you do? Spend four hours a day in the gym?"

Beckett smothered a laugh.

Her hands slid down between them, digging into his abs. The muscles there contracted against the pleasure of her touch. He wanted more. Craved it, as much as any drug. "You should be illegal. How am I supposed to resist you?"

She pulled back, staring straight into his eyes. "God, you're beautiful."

"Men don't like to be called beautiful, either, sweetheart," Beckett whispered, his voice gravelly with suppressed need.

"But you are."

Desperate for some separation before his control crumbled completely, Beckett let her body slither down his until her feet hit the floor. He'd planned to back away, but the moment he tried she staggered sideways.

That, more than anything, worked to clear the fog of arousal invading his brain.

Putting his hands on her shoulders, Beckett pushed gently until her body folded and she sat on the side of the bed. The skirt she was wearing flared around her hips, leaving her thighs half-bare. She didn't seem to notice or care.

Beckett knelt at her feet, reaching to undo the straps on her sandals. The memory of their first encounter flashed through his mind, her bent over a long creamy thigh, unbuckling another shoe.

Not helping. Not helping at all, he admonished his brain.

Alyssa leaned toward him, running her hands over his shoulders and down his back. Her fingertips found the hem of his shirt and slipped beneath.

He sucked a sharp breath through his teeth. His hands tightened, one around her calf and the other at her ankle. Part of him worried he was hurting her, but it was either that or push her backward and give in to the need racing through him.

"You have to stop that," he ground out on a guttural groan.

"Why?" she asked, her voice slow and dreamy.

"Because you don't know what you're doing." Reaching behind him, he untangled her fingers and brought them to her knees. And held them in place with the weight of his own.

"I'm hanging on by a thread, princess. Help me out before we both do something we'll regret."

Misery flashed through her eyes, cutting him straight to the bone. "You'd regret sleeping with me? I suppose I shouldn't be surprised. Why would a few years make any difference?"

"Hell, no," he said in a low rumble. "From the moment I saw you on that balcony, I've thought of nothing *but* having you. I don't want *you* to regret it. Even if you probably won't remember any of this in the morning."

Beckett didn't realize what he'd said—and revealed—until the words were out of his mouth. But by then it was too late to take them back. Although Alyssa didn't seem to notice. She was focused solely on the fact that he did want her.

Beckett couldn't stop the feeling of relief—and guilt—that flooded him.

Insistent fingers back at his shirt, she begged, "I want to touch you. Please, let me touch you. If I won't remember then there's no harm in letting go and giving in to what I want."

Hearing her say she wanted him as much as he wanted her was more temptation than he could beat back.

Lifting his arms high into the air, he let her pull the shirt over his head. But that was all he was losing. And she was keeping every stitch of clothing on.

Teasing fingertips ghosted across his skin, dipped into the valleys of his abs and smoothed across his ribs. Sharp, white teeth dug into the tempting flesh of her lower lip. He wanted to tug it free. To soothe the marks she was putting there and taste the sweetness of her mouth.

But he didn't trust himself that far.

So he knelt there, propped up on his heels, and let her explore. Groaning, he closed his eyes and let his head drop back in pure ecstasy.

This was as much torture as watching her strip and knowing he couldn't touch. No, this was worse. She was right here. Willing and eager. And still, he couldn't have her.

As far as torture tactics went, this was far beyond anything ever devised.

Was it wrong that he hoped she'd pass out soon? And prayed she wouldn't?

God, it was going to be a long night.

6

ALYSSA'S BUZZER SOUNDED and Megan's muffled voice followed. "Let me in before I drop this big-ass box!"

After last night, she'd expected Megan to show at some point. According to her phone, Alyssa had sent Megan a text letting her know her drink had been spiked and Beckett was taking her home, but her friend wouldn't be content with those few words. She was nosy and would want the full-blown explanation.

Unfortunately, Alyssa couldn't remember what had happened. Anxiety and embarrassment twisted through her gut. She'd woken up in Beckett's guest room. Alone. Still wearing all of her clothes, which was a good thing.

She had a few fuzzy memories. Being pissed at those guys, upset when Beckett insisted on taking her to his place. And maybe…possibly…running her fingers along his naked skin. Although, it was entirely possible that had been a dream.

When she'd stumbled into his kitchen this morning, bleary-eyed and disoriented, he'd handed her a cup of coffee and immediately promised her nothing had happened and that his neighbor said she'd be fine.

She hated herself a little for the disappointment she'd felt.

With nothing else to do, she'd thanked Beckett for taking care of her, refused his offer to drive her home and called a cab as soon as she could.

Even now, the memory of those moments laden with tension made her skin heat. She'd gotten the awkward morning after with none of the mind-blowing enjoyment from the night before.

Part of her felt robbed.

Groaning, Alyssa punched the button that would let Megan in. Better to get this over with now. Her head still fuzzy from the drug, she'd called into the office. Staring at lines of code probably wouldn't have been a smart decision.

Megan, her face and half of her body concealed behind a huge gold box, tumbled inside Alyssa's apartment. She kicked the door closed behind her, tottered into the kitchen and dropped the thing onto the counter.

"What the heck is that?" Alyssa asked, eyeing the box suspiciously. It had to be at least three feet long and two feet wide.

"How should I know?" Running her hands through pale blond hair, Megan pushed the wispy strands away from her face. "It's yours, not mine. Courier arrived downstairs as I came in. Figured I'd save you the trip down."

This just got stranger and stranger. Alyssa's hands slid across the surface of the box. It was slick and shiny, closed with a deep burgundy ribbon tied into a perfect, stiff bow.

Was it wrong that she got a little thrill when she looked at it? Hoped it was from her masked stranger? She hadn't heard anything from him in almost three days and the silence was killing her.

Especially with visions of Beckett Kayne crowding her brain. She didn't want them there. Didn't want him there. How mixed up was it that a masked stranger felt safer than a man she actually knew?

She eyed the box. Christmas and birthdays had never been her favorite occasions. While her sister had opened a pile of presents so big you could barely see her behind them, Alyssa had only received a handful. And it wasn't that she wasn't grateful. But compared to the expensive electronics, beautiful clothes and glittering jewelry Mercedes had been lavished with, the functional and practical gifts she'd received were a slap in the face.

She'd always ended those days with an ache lodged straight in the center of her chest. The thing was, she hadn't even really wanted the things Mercedes squealed over. She'd just wanted her dad to care enough to notice the difference.

Sometime in her early teens she'd begun to realize that bone-deep wish would never come true. So she'd made the best of what she had, drawing out the anticipation and playing a little game in her head.

Picking up the box, she said, "It's light," with surprise. Megan had staggered in like it harbored an elephant.

"Yeah, but the sucker was a bitch to carry." Megan glared at the box. "Having short arms sucks."

Alyssa laughed, unable to keep the bubble of excitement from slipping out. She shouldn't. She knew better. But there it was.

"Considering the box is almost bigger than you—"

"Bite me," Megan countered with a feral grin that only made Alyssa want to laugh harder.

Megan barely topped out at five feet. She was tiny and slender, and her pale, short hair, pointed chin and wide blue eyes only added to the ethereal air that clung to her. Guys fell over themselves to take care of her. The thing was, she might look fragile, but she actually had a backbone of steel.

Beside her, Megan grumbled something incoherent. Grabbing the glass of wine out of Alyssa's hand, she drank the entire thing in one gulp, then gave her a look full of expectation and barely checked annoyance. "Well, are you going to open it?"

"Yeah," Alyssa answered, still staring at it as if she might suddenly develop the ability to see inside. "In a minute."

Taking a deep breath, she picked up the box and shook it. A faint rustling sounded and then a muffled thunk. The side of the box reverberated with the impact of something hard.

"What the heck was that?" Megan asked.

Alyssa just shrugged. Until that thunk she would have bet money the box contained clothes of some kind. She'd gotten enough socks, underwear and god-awful sweaters in her life to know the sound of material sliding against cardboard. The last sound intrigued her and made her little guessing game that much harder.

She tilted the box the other direction and waited for the same rasping slide and smack.

Getting impatient, Megan reached for the box and tried to rip it out of her hands. "For God's sake, if you're not going to open it I will. I'm dying to know what's inside. Aren't you?"

She was. But she was also enjoying the anticipation…

and the fantasy that her masked, mystery man was the one who had sent the surprise.

Jerking it up and out of Megan's reach, Alyssa glared down at her. "My pretty," she scolded even as a silly, playful grin stretched her lips.

Megan just huffed and crossed her arms over her chest to wait. They both knew that without climbing onto the bar stool beside her Megan would never reach the box. Alyssa had at least six inches on her…without her heels.

Excitement swelling inside her chest to the point she wasn't sure she could stand it anymore, Alyssa finally set the box back on the counter and tugged at the ends of the bow. The ribbon slithered silently away. She lifted the lid and didn't even look where it landed when she flicked a wrist and sent it sailing behind her.

Spreading back layers of tissue paper so thin she could practically see through them, she stared down at what lay inside. Not in a million years would she have guessed this.

Megan let out a gasp quickly followed by the kind of girlie sigh that could convey so much.

Alyssa swallowed, unwanted tears pricking her eyes. It was beautiful. Possibly the most beautiful present she'd ever received. Which was sad on so many levels, but she refused to focus on that truth. She wouldn't let her melancholy thoughts ruin the moment.

Nestled inside was a dress. No, a costume. The material was so delicate and airy it almost appeared to float. Her fingers slipped across it. Soft. Maybe silk, although it had to be extremely expensive to be that thin and fragile. Even the colors were light and subtle. Shades of shimmery blue, purple and black.

The colors almost perfectly matched the fairy tattooed across her right ribs. Her belly fluttered.

Reinforcing the thought, nestled behind the dress was a set of fairy wings, the same material as the dress stretched over metal bent into the right shape.

Her fingers trailed along the material. He'd seen. Remembered. And given her a costume that matched the picture she'd permanently etched into her skin. A tingle spread from her fingers, across her shoulders and down her chest to settle into a deep ache right at the center of her body.

It wasn't just arousal, although that was part of it. It was hard not to anticipate him taking her out of the breathtaking dress. But it was more. A ball of bliss that was scary in its intensity.

It had been a very long time since anything had made her this happy. And it was seriously dangerous that a stranger had given her the experience.

Alyssa didn't exactly trust happiness. In her experience it never lasted long. Something always, *always* screwed it up.

And given the complicated, crazy situation, there were so many options for how this could go terribly wrong.

Swallowing, Alyssa forced her hands out of the box. She took a step away from the temptation it represented.

Megan, oblivious to her sudden change of attitude, reached inside and pulled out a silvery sandal. Thin, glitter-encrusted straps crisscrossed up to a thick band that would probably hit just above her ankle. The heels were spindly and at least four inches high. And the sole was bloodred.

With a reverent sigh, Megan held it high as if making an offering to the shoe gods. "I'd kill for these. Seriously, if we wore the same size you'd already be on the floor bleeding."

Alyssa chuckled, the wheezing sound just the release she needed for the pent-up angst storming her body.

"And who, pray tell, has sent you a box full of goodies that probably cost a couple thousand dollars?"

Alyssa's eyes widened. Surely Megan had to be wrong.

Carefully replacing the shoe, Megan snatched the cream-colored envelope with Alyssa's name scrawled across it in precise letters. She should probably stop Megan, but she wanted to know just as badly as her friend.

To fill her hands, Alyssa picked up the mask that had been sitting beside the envelope. The mask was the same shades of blue, purple and black, the holes for her eyes studded with glittering rhinestones. The bottom edge dropped down into two swirling curlicues that would cover half her cheekbones. The top half matched, the swirls most likely tall enough to thrust into her hairline. A thread of silvery glitter snaked across the whole thing.

Alyssa stood there, staring, unable to move or think or breathe. This was the kind of thing that happened to other women. Or fairy-tale princesses. She was not the woman who received gorgeous, expensive, anonymous gifts.

She was the woman no one noticed.

There was no way, in that dress, anyone would be able to ignore her.

A longing, sharp and hard, slammed into her. It threatened to consume her, choke her, devour her beneath the weight of a wish she'd spent years convincing herself didn't exist.

No, she would not do this. She wouldn't let herself

hope. The crushing disappointment was never worth the brief few moments of weightless wonder.

She'd refuse it. Send it back.

She was about to grab the lid, close the box and order Megan to put it in the hall when Megan popped the flap on the envelope and pulled out a heavy piece of vellum.

Another paper fluttered to the counter, ignored by both of them as Megan's blue eyes darted across what was obviously an invitation.

"Oh, my God," she breathed out with a burst of giddy awe that sent a shiver of unease straight through Alyssa.

Turning her gaze, Megan asked, "Do you know what this is?"

Obviously she didn't. She hadn't read it. Shaking her head, Alyssa leaned closer so that she could see. The words scratched onto the surface of the expensive paper had been hand penned in calligraphy.

"I've only heard rumors about this ball, Lys. Not from anyone who's actually been. You know, the friend of a friend of a cousin's boyfriend kind of thing. It's very hush-hush."

Megan's gaze collided with hers, full of divine worship with a healthy dose of jealousy mixed in for fun. "How did you score an invitation? And at the last minute."

"I have…" Alyssa had to take a second to clear her throat. "I have no idea."

"Hair. Makeup. Now. According to this you have less than two hours to get ready."

Megan was practically vibrating with excitement as she bolted through Alyssa's apartment, disappearing into her bedroom.

"Wait. What?" Alyssa cried, trailing helplessly behind her friend. "I'm not going."

From her bathroom, Megan let out a loud laugh. "Of course you're going. No one turns down an invite to the Bacchanalia Ball. No one."

"But…" Alyssa sputtered. "But I can't be ready in time. This is too much. Too fast."

Megan's head poked out around the door, her pointed features pulled into a hard glare. "You are not using that as an excuse. We have just enough time for me to fix your face and hair."

Alyssa didn't have time to play dress up. She had too much on her mind. Too much to do. And the fact that her chest was so tight she was struggling to drag in a single full breath only told her she was making the right decision.

These kinds of things didn't happen to her.

But it was too late. She could already hear Megan making herself at home, clanging through her bathroom drawers. Whenever she got in this kind of whirlwind there was no stopping her. Normally, Alyssa liked that about Megan. It made her efficient and unstoppable. Although this was the first time that determination had been directed squarely against her own intentions.

Retracing her steps, Alyssa sank down onto a barstool. The uncomfortable fluttering in her stomach increased.

The white paper that had slipped from the envelope caught her attention. Without thinking, she reached for it. Her fingers smoothed over the surface, pinching it open and revealing more of the same scrawling handwriting that had graced the outside of the envelope.

Masculine and sharp, there were no wasted strokes or pretentious embellishments on the words. No calligraphy for him. Nope, the handwriting and the words themselves were quick and direct. Just like the man who'd sent them.

Tonight you wear the mask.
And only what's inside the box.
Tonight neither of us walks away unsatisfied.

How HAD SHE gotten herself into this mess?

Alyssa stared down at the dress, a combination of horror, excitement and fevered need twisting deep inside. There was a sinful expanse of skin on display. Her skin.

Inside the box the dress had looked like a dream. And it still was. The only difference was that apparently the fairy tale she was starring in would be rated R. Or possibly NC-17.

Just what the heck happened at this ball?

Megan couldn't tell her, which did nothing to soothe her steadily increasing nerves. Megan had spent an hour curling, sculpting and pinning Alyssa's hair up into the kind of artful style that was supposed to look as though it was effortless and might come tumbling down in the first stiff breeze. The ache at the back of her head was evidence it wasn't going anywhere. She could swear Megan had jabbed several of the damn pins straight through her skull.

Her nails were painted a soft, shimmery purple that matched her dress and the eye makeup that had taken twenty minutes to perfect.

Several times during the torture she'd changed her mind and almost ordered Megan to stop the madness. But each time she was tempted, the words on that white page would flash across her mind.

Tonight she'd find out who he really was. She was wearing the mask, which implied he wouldn't. And he'd promised neither of them would leave unfulfilled. The sharp ache that had been pulsing between her thighs since the moment she'd turned and noticed him watching her from the shadows ratcheted up one more notch. Much more and she was going to explode.

Her palms smoothed down the gossamer-soft material again. She couldn't seem to stop stroking it.

Really, she rationalized, the dress wasn't as scandalous as she'd first thought. Yes, it was a little more…transparent than she would have normally worn, but everything essential was covered.

Layers of material floated around her body, sweeping the floor. Picking one up, she held it in front of her, her palm spread wide beneath it. It was so sheer a palmist could have told her fortune.

The variation of color was achieved by adding one section atop another. Several were bunched together into flimsy ropes of material. They crossed over her chest, slashed diagonally across her abdomen and arched over her hips.

Starting just below her belly button, curving up slightly at the hip and then dipping back down at the small of her back, several shorter layers of material were added to the others. They were barely long enough to skim a few inches down her thighs, but they kept her from flashing her hoo-ha and butt cheeks at everyone.

There hadn't been a bra or panties in the box, something she hadn't registered until she started dressing. Although, even if they had been inside she wasn't sure they'd have done any good. Not caring what the note said, she'd pulled out her skimpiest pair of panties and put them on. The waistband had been visible above the line of the skirt and they'd given her a hell of a panty line in the back.

So she'd removed them again, the knowledge that she'd

be walking into an exclusive ball bare underneath the sensuous dress ratcheting up her already taut nerves. Taking a deep breath, Alyssa looked into the mirror. She stared hard into her own eyes. Okay, decision time. Was she doing this or not?

She'd never been the girl to take risks with her personal life. In business she was confident and undaunted. Outside the boardroom...

It was difficult to shut off the little voice inside her head that sneered *what will everyone think?* It probably wasn't a coincidence that the voice sounded strangely like her stepmother.

She hadn't worried about anyone's opinion when she'd stripped for her masked stranger. Yes, there was a level of safety there, being in her own apartment above a controlled access alley. But that safety net hadn't been in place when she'd let him kiss and touch her in the middle of a crowded street.

Both of those experiences had thrilled her. The only disappointment she'd experienced with him was when it had ended.

Tonight she was masked, so there was a layer of anonymity...protection. Enough to make her feel safe. Or maybe that was the thought of being in *his* arms again.

As far as risks went, the situation actually held very few. The biggest one being the level of her own craving. It scared her how much she wanted this man. This stranger. How much she burned for his touch.

On the bright side, maybe if she went through with this, the irrational attraction she had for Kayne would disappear.

That alone made the danger worth it.

Decision made, she grabbed the silver handbag Megan

had found in her closet and sauntered to the door. In the heels with straps so fragile she feared they might disintegrate right off her feet, and a dress she was afraid would swirl up at the barest hint of a breeze and reveal every feminine secret she possessed, she couldn't do anything *but* saunter.

Slipping the mask on, she grabbed the wings. She didn't want to crush them in the cab so wouldn't put them on until she got there. Pushing out onto the sidewalk, she was surprised to see a man clad in a white shirt, black suit and chauffeur's cap.

"Ms. Vaughn?" he asked politely.

Alyssa simply nodded.

He led her to a dark car parked around the corner. She wasn't going to ask how he'd gotten through the Fat Tuesday crowd. Opening the car door, he gestured her inside and waited expectantly.

She was in trouble. Serious trouble.

A girl could get used to this. And get her heart crushed when the spellbinding fable crashed back into drab reality.

7

He knew the moment she arrived. And not just because James, the driver he'd hired for the night, had texted him when she'd left the car.

The air shifted. Growing heavier, it pressed against his chest with the weight of anticipation and uncertainty.

He had no idea what she'd do when she figured out who he was. Would she run? Yell? Helplessly melt against him?

He was hoping for option three, but was prepared for the other two. They were more likely.

He couldn't envision Alyssa Vaughn simply accepting a complication like this with calm silence. She was going to have to work through it, but he needed her to know it was him behind the mask.

Three nights later and he still couldn't get the taste of her off his tongue. She was constantly there, sweet and sharp. And the feel of her hands running over his chest...

Last night it had taken everything inside him not to follow through on what he wanted. She'd been in his home. In his bed. Warm and willing.

But if that had been hard, seeing her this morning had

been torture. Especially knowing what he already had planned for tonight. She'd been rumpled, her skin flushed warm, and her eyes had been blessedly clear, the drug purged from her system.

However, her restless awkwardness had kept him on his side of the kitchen, doing nothing more than watching as she sucked down a cup of black coffee. Letting her walk away had been agonizing.

From his position on a balcony overlooking the entrance to the ballroom, he watched her enter. It was a good thing he was already holding on to the railing, because the sight of her nearly sent him to his knees.

Her heavy hair had been pulled to the crown of her head in a mass of curls that begged him to thrust his fingers in deep and send the silken mass tumbling across his hands. Most of her face was hidden, but her mouth was pink and glossy and eminently kissable.

The need to taste her again whipped through him, punishing and relentless. His fingers curled around the hard edge of the wooden barrier, anchoring him in place. He needed to get a grip. Engage his head before he did something stupid and screwed up everything.

One wrong move and she'd bolt. He'd had enough of a glimpse inside that complicated, intriguing mind of hers last night to realize that if that happened it would be all over. She wouldn't give him a second chance.

The body she loved to cover with those conservative business clothes was clearly on display. He'd known the dress was perfect for her the moment he'd seen it. It wasn't the most daring outfit that would grace the masquerade, but it was enough to unsettle her…and if he'd read her right, set her heart racing with heightened awareness and arousal.

Alyssa Vaughn had an exhibitionistic streak that made him ache. And he was going to enjoy proving to her there was nothing wrong with giving in to the fantasy. Starting tonight.

She moved several feet into the room, her gaze sweeping across the crowd. At the moment it was staid. Later in the evening—after alcohol had flowed freely, inhibitions had been dropped and desires rose to the surface— things would get crazy.

Stopping on the fringes of the crowd, she paused to take everything in. He'd attended his first ball when he was in his early twenties, his contacts in the club scene gaining him entrance.

Trying to remember back that far, he wondered if he'd had the same wide-eyed, innocent reaction that not even Alyssa's mask could hide. He didn't think so. Perhaps he'd already been too jaded by then. Tonight she gave him a gift she wasn't even aware of, letting him experience the moment through her.

The room was bathed in candlelight, the guests preferring the shadowy atmosphere it provided. What little light there was shimmered off crystal and gold chandeliers. Everywhere things sparkled. Jewels, costumes, champagne flutes, gold-rimmed plates and inlaid silverware.

Eyes followed her as she pushed through the crowd, heading for the balcony rimming the room. She'd apparently realized the best vantage point would be from up high.

He'd chosen this spot purposefully. Surely what they'd started on a balcony should be finished on one, as well.

Weaving through the bodies, she left a trail of men staring in her wake and was completely unaware of her effect. Several of them waited for a single sign that she was open for approach, but when none came they turned away. One or two of the bolder men ignored her silent signals, brushing against her, holding her in place and leaning close to speak.

He tried not to let the way she instinctively pulled away from their advances matter. But he couldn't stop a flood of satisfaction.

Slamming back the last of his Macallan, Beckett placed the empty glass on a table. Positioned at the farthest end of the balcony, he melted into the dark shadows and waited for her to come to him.

Blue and purple flashes, and glimpses of the skin beneath, tempted him as she walked slowly down the length of the balcony. It took everything in him to stand still and watch.

Up here, the sumptuous decor continued: flickering candlelight; plush, wine-red carpeting; glinting gold fixtures and gleaming wrought-iron and dark wood railings. Columns were interspersed along the space, holding up the ceiling and providing a few pockets of privacy.

She drifted past him, her eyes trained on the crowd beneath her instead of at the darkness behind. The moment her scent—something sweet and subtle but undeniably hers—assaulted him, it was all over. The last shred of his resistance shattered.

It was like waving a red flag in front of a bull and not expecting him to charge.

She reached the far end of the balcony and paused. On silent feet, he approached. His hands settled on her shoulders as he turned her to face him.

Instinct had her moving to jerk out of his hold, but the moment her gaze met his, her body stilled. Then she leaned closer into him. That, more than anything, settled the nerves rippling through him.

She ran her fingers over the mask he wore. Stark black silk that matched his suit, it was different from the one she was used to.

"I thought you weren't wearing this tonight." Her voice was low, sultry, a murmur just for his ears.

"Everyone wears a mask tonight."

Her pale-green eyes stared straight into him. Unblinking and unwavering. There was no hesitation, only a dull flash of disappointment. She *wanted* to know who he was. At least, a part of her did, although he knew there was also something that excited her about not knowing. She rode the edge of the conflicting urges.

Slowly, her fingers trailed along the mask, over his cheekbones, the upper curve of his ears and into his hair. Her fingertips smoothed the string holding his mask in place. Tight knots squeezed harder in the pit of his gut, but he didn't make a move.

This was her choice.

ALYSSA STARED UP into stormy blue eyes. His body was still, although she could feel the coiled tension filling each of his muscles.

Did she want to know? Or did she want to give in to the mindless need storming her? And deal with the rest later.

She knew what her body wanted, even if her mind was shouting at her to be smart. But she'd spent so much of her life being careful. Making sure she said and did the right thing because she was afraid one mistake would destroy the little security she had.

But being perfect hadn't saved her from the pain of

countless small slights and verbal cuts. What had she missed out on, constantly worrying about how her decisions and actions might reflect on her father?

There was no reason to hesitate, not anymore.

Tonight was for her and her alone. To hell with what anyone else thought. Anyone aside from her masked stranger.

This man made her feel alive in a way no one else ever had. She wanted him. This. The way he made her feel, whole and right and free. Some instinct told her that the moment his mask came off everything between them would change. The fantasy would disappear and she'd have to live with reality.

She wasn't ready for that. But she also wasn't willing to just fold like a house of cards.

The man had dressed her up like some X-rated doll and then let her wander the ballroom, waiting for him to materialize. She'd felt the weight of his eyes on her, watching, letting her nerves wind higher and higher as she searched him out in the writhing crowd.

She wasn't one for games, but that's all they'd been doing together. Although, she had to admit, he wasn't the only one playing. Hadn't she done the same thing their first night?

She should snap the string and end this. But she just… couldn't.

"Turn around," he said, his deep voice melting over her like the best hot caramel. Just like ice cream, she could imagine herself melting into a gooey puddle beneath the weight of that voice. Especially if he used it to growl naughty things in her ear as she came.

Not that she did what he'd asked.

Alyssa desperately tried to find her sense of self-preservation. She obviously never should have put on this dress tonight. It had drained her of all inhibitions.

As if he could read her thoughts, a dangerous glint sparked inside his dark blue eyes, shielded by shadows and the mask. There was something about them…something familiar, but before she could pinpoint the niggling thought her attention was drawn to his mouth.

His lips twitched as if he was holding back a smile.

"Are you laughing at me?" she breathed out, inexplicable alarm clamoring through her. The ghost of sneering laughter whispered across her mind. Nasty words. *Tramp, slut, whore.*

Her body went tense. She tried to pull away, to hide, but he wouldn't let her.

The heat of his hold shifted from her shoulders, trailing softly down over her back to settle just where her spine dipped in. He didn't haul her closer, instead he held her steady and came to her, invading her space surely and completely.

His mouth brushed against the shell of her ear and a sharp tingle lanced straight between her thighs.

"Absolutely not. There's nothing about this that's funny, Alyssa. You have me tied in knots. At your mercy. I've never wanted a woman as much as I want you."

His words and touch soothed her, although they couldn't completely banish the terrible thoughts, now that they'd invaded. Apprehension, a little late to the party, flowed through her. From somewhere far away she heard her own voice whisper belated words of sanity, "This is a bad idea."

"Hmm," he said, the vibration of the sound trembling through her.

With nothing more than a shift of his body, he rubbed

against her, delicious friction that sent tingles scattering across her skin. She was tall and with the high-heeled shoes she'd been practically at eye level with most of the men here tonight. But not him. Oh, no. He had her beat by at least three inches.

And he knew how to use them, looming over her and leaving her no choice but to arch back.

His mouth touched her ear and a ripple of goose bumps spread across her neck and chest. "I'm curious to discover, Alyssa, did you follow instructions?"

She sucked in a hard breath. The room seemed to spin, the only thing keeping her up the anchoring weight of his palm pressed between her wings. Something soft brushed her thigh. It took her several moments to realize it was his fingers, not touching her, but slowly gathering the gossamer skirt into a bunch.

Her concentration cracked. She could think about nothing else as he wound the material higher and higher on her thigh. In a moment he would expose her, the wall of his body the only shield to keep anyone from seeing.

Why did that knowledge send the passion rioting through her into a frenzy?

His heat suffused her, enveloped her. Overwhelmed her. She wanted more. Needed to feel the slide of his fingers over her, not just through the barrier of her dress.

After days of wondering and fantasizing he was so close....

Anticipation sparked just beneath the surface of her skin.

His lips trailed across the line of her jaw. Her fists bunched his stark white shirt, clinging to anything that would keep her upright. Her legs trembled.

She couldn't catch her breath. She was drowning, unable to make the smallest move to save herself. All she had to do was step away from him. But she couldn't.

He teased her, kissing her nose, her eyes, both cheeks and the dimple at the center of her chin. He nibbled each corner of her mouth and licked the dent just above her upper lip.

God, she wanted him to kiss her. Her lips parted. A soft whimper slipped out.

At her back, his fingers spasmed, going wide and then contracting hard as if he couldn't get a tight enough hold on her.

Right before he gave her what she wanted, he growled against her mouth, "Are you wearing only what was inside the box?"

It was an assault—the kiss, his wicked words. They worked together, spinning dangerously. Building her desire and dismantling her defenses.

Her mind emptied of everything but the way he made her feel.

Hot. Desperate. Exposed.

There was nothing soft about the kiss. It was an all-out invasion. His tongue thrust deep inside, demanding. She parried and tangled. Nipped and groaned. Plucked at the shirt beneath her hands, trying to find a way inside.

His own hands roamed across her body, never settling in one place long enough to soothe the ache building inside. In some tangled corner of her brain, she registered his nimble fingers pulling at the bands connecting the wings to her back. She didn't realize the weight of them until they were gone, simply discarded at their feet and abandoned.

She forgot everything, especially that they were standing in an occupied ballroom. Nothing mattered except touching him. More of him. As much as she could get at.

He was the one to pull back. She moaned a protest.

She was dazed. Reeling. Unable to do anything but stare up into his dark eyes. The intense heat staring back at her should have blistered her skin. She could feel the energy of his need vibrating just beneath the surface. His jaw was tight, his muscles hard, his control held by the thinnest thread.

And all she could think about was what it would take to snap it. To make him mindless and desperate…just as she was.

But before she could form a plan, she was spinning. Her waist pressed against the balcony railing. His body settled behind her, the heat of him spilling into her senses. His palms, placed beside her own, curled around the wooden edge, caging her in.

Her mind fuzzy, she stood there, desperately trying to make her world stop spiraling, when a horn trumpeted through the room and her entire body jolted.

"What's going on?" she asked, a little dazed.

"The thiasus. The procession. The masquerade is a tribute to Bacchus," he said, with a shrug she could feel more than see, as if that explained everything.

"Watch," he whispered against her skin.

Although he didn't touch her, the warmth of his body did, overwhelming her. His scent, something sharp, masculine and clean, filled her lungs. She could feel him. So close, and yet not close enough. Her lips tingled, remembering his touch and wanting more than the powerful caresses he'd just given.

Swallowing, Alyssa tried to ignore her reaction and concentrate on what was happening below. Megan would pump her for info tomorrow so she needed to pay attention. And use these moments to try to recover her sanity.

A wide line had been cleared through the center of the ballroom. For the first time, Alyssa noticed a huge dais at the far end of the space. Would a band be playing later? If so, she didn't see any instruments or equipment. Instead, there was a single, high-backed chair with elegant scrollwork. An array of large pillows littered the floor. There had to be at least twenty or thirty in every shade of the rainbow.

There were tables, several of them, groaning beneath the weight of platters of food. And in the center, placed right next to the throne, was a large fountain, deep red wine flowing through it.

But before she could think about it more, a round of applause erupted through the crowd. It started at the far end and swept across the room. The air seemed to shift, excitement rolling up at her.

Dancers pranced out into the open. Alyssa watched them move, their bodies lithe and graceful. Arms waved in large, grand gestures. Feet pointed. Legs kicked high. Small leaps. Intricate turns. Backs arching and then sweeping forward. Hips rolling. They were gorgeous, all twelve of them.

She was so taken by their movements that it was several moments before she realized the women were… naked. Well, not quite. They were draped from head to toe in gold—chains, bracelets, cuffs, beads. Around their waists, down to their navels, up arms and legs. The sway of metal and decoration moved with their bodies. At first she'd assumed they wore *something* beneath the weight of all the jewelry.

She was wrong. And knew it when the procession

moved closer. One of the dancer's draping chains parted and Alyssa got a prolonged flash of naked breast. The swell of skin was pale, but the large circle of areola was a dark rose. And the dancer's nipple was puckered so tight and hard it made Alyssa's own ache.

She hadn't noticed her stranger's hand move, not until his thumb and finger settled right over her breast and tugged gently. Alyssa's head jerked back, colliding with the hard wall of his chest. Her body instinctively arched into his touch, begging for more.

He teased, his fingers somehow finding a way beneath the layers of cloth to her bare flesh. Biting back a groan, Alyssa tried to fight the reaction, but it was a losing battle. She'd done nothing but torture herself with fantasies of her masked stranger touching her.

But her brain tried to mount a last-ditch effort at caution, screaming for her to put some distance between them. She tried to turn away, but strong, steady hands held her fast, keeping her in place. "Watch," he whispered, the sweep of his breath hot and heavy against her sensitized skin.

"What if someone's watching *us?*" she asked, anxiety and anticipation coloring her words.

His lips ghosted across the nape of her neck, a barely there caress that only had her craving more. "But that's what you like, Alyssa. It fires your blood, excites you. And I have to admit, the idea of other men watching you, wanting you, all while knowing you can only think of my hands on your body…it's sexy as hell. I promise to protect you. I'd never let anyone hurt you. I won't do anything you don't want. All you have to do is say stop, and I will."

She nodded, understanding and acknowledging what he'd just said. Perhaps she shouldn't trust his words…but she did. Instinctively she knew the moment she balked this would all be over.

But she didn't want it to be.

And, really, her words were a lie. Oh, a part of her was concerned about being seen. She was too much a product of her father's admonishments not to have that tiny voice in the back of her head.

But if she was honest, with herself and him, there was something she was more worried about. Digging deep to find the courage, she forced out the words in a breathy voice. "What happens when you get what you want?"

He dragged a fingernail across the aching tip of her breast, and Alyssa's thighs clenched against the sharp sting of arousal that arrowed straight to her sex as she waited for his answer. How was she supposed to think when her body was rebelling against her?

"What do you think will happen, Alyssa?"

"That you'll walk away. Taking that mask and your anonymity, disappearing back into the crowd, never to be seen again."

Crushing her tight, aching nipples between thumb and forefinger, he pinched. She gasped, her eyelids fluttering closed at the flood of pleasure spiked with pain. But it was only there for a moment, immediately soothed away by the teasing, tugging sensation of him playing with her. He measured the weight of her breasts in his palms, holding and massaging. A matching hollow weight settled deep inside her, throbbing and pulsing out her need.

His mouth, tongue and teeth seared a trail down her nape. "I'm not going anywhere, Alyssa. Trust me, one night with you will be far from enough." He punctuated the confession by sinking a love bite into the spot right at the bend of her shoulder.

FREE Merchandise is 'in the Cards' for you!

Dear Reader,

We're giving away FREE MERCHANDISE!

Seriously, we'd like to reward you for reading this novel by giving you **FREE MERCHANDISE** worth over $20. And no purchase is necessary!

You see the Jack of Hearts sticker above? Paste that sticker in the box on the Free Merchandise Voucher inside. Return the Voucher promptly...and we'll send you valuable Free Merchandise!

Thanks again for reading one of our novels—and enjoy your Free Merchandise with our compliments!

Pam Powers

Pam Powers

P.S. Look inside to see what Free Merchandise is **"in the cards"** for you!

We'd like to send you two free books like the one you are enjoying now. Your two books have a combined price of over $10, but they are yours to keep absolutely FREE! We'll even send you 2 wonderful surprise gifts. You can't lose!

HARLEQUIN Blaze

Still So Hot!

Serena Bell

HARLEQUIN Blaze

My Secret Fantasies

FORBIDDEN FANTASIES

Joanne Rock

REMEMBER: Your Free Merchandise, consisting of **2 Free Books** and **2 Free Gifts**, is worth over $20.00! No purchase is necessary, so please send for your Free Merchandise today.

Get TWO FREE GIFTS!

We'll also send you two wonderful FREE GIFTS (worth about $10), in addition to your 2 Free books!

Visit us at:
www.ReaderService.com

YOUR FREE MERCHANDISE INCLUDES...
2 FREE Books **AND** 2 FREE Mystery Gifts

FREE MERCHANDISE VOUCHER

2 FREE BOOKS
and
2 FREE GIFTS

Please send my Free Merchandise, consisting of
2 Free Books and **2 Free Mystery Gifts**.
I understand that I am under no obligation to buy
anything, as explained on the back of this card.

150/350 HDL GEC7

Please Print

FIRST NAME

LAST NAME

ADDRESS

APT.#   CITY

STATE/PROV.   ZIP/POSTAL CODE

NO PURCHASE NECESSARY!

HB_314_FM13

In that moment, all of her concerns melted. There was only one thing she wanted—for him to take her away to someplace private and stop teasing her.

They were both acting as if there'd been a decision to make. Hadn't she made it already by coming here in the first place?

She might regret the decision, but there would be plenty of time for that later. Right now she wanted to feel. The last shred of fight draining from her body, she sagged against him.

And he caught her, holding tight and wrapping his arms around her as if she was made of fragile glass. But he didn't take her away. Instead, he cupped her chin and returned her focus to the spectacle below. "Watch."

The dancers had settled on the dais, draping their bodies across the pillows as if they were being presented as precious gifts. Servers materialized beside them, offering wine and food. They indulged, somehow giving the impression of gluttonous abandonment.

More movement caught Alyssa's attention and she jerked her gaze back across the room. Another group entered, twenty men. At least they were clothed, although they might as well not have bothered.

Their chests, clearly oiled, gleamed in the muted light. While every shade—white, brown, black, tan—was represented, their physiques matched. Wide shoulders, tapered waists and the kind of muscular definition that would make any woman's body thud with appreciation.

Several of the women—and a few men—in the audience reached out, running their hands along the display of male flesh as they stalked past. It bothered her, until she realized the men didn't seem to care.

Gold cuffs circled every wrist. Their black shorts were

so tight there was practically nothing left to the imagination.

Suddenly, her masked stranger's hips surged forward.
She hadn't realized he'd been holding himself away from
her, not until the hot, hard length of him pressed against
the small of her back.

A burning wave of need exploded through her body,
leaving her flustered and flushed from head to toe.

With the pressure of his hand between her shoulder
blades he urged her to bend at the waist. Her body draped
over the railing. He stayed with her, following her down.
The change in position shifted his cock lower, just shy
of the throbbing entrance to her body. He was so close…
pulsing, teasing and making her that much more desperate.

His movement forced soft material across her skin,
the dress becoming a caress all its own. Somehow a couple of pieces had been caught between her body and the
railing. With each surge the silk tugged and teased her
swollen, sensitive sex.

If he didn't stop she was going to explode just from
that. And that's not what she wanted. She wanted him.
Craved him in a way that she'd never experienced.

But that didn't stop her from pushing her hips back
into him, using the leverage of the railing to get more.

The men finally settled on the dais, intertwining with
the women already on display. Several poured wine into
each other's open mouths. Or licked it off skin. Some fed
each other. Others didn't bother with the pretense and
blatantly stroked and fondled. It was a naked display of
wanton excess. And Alyssa couldn't pull her eyes away.

Another trumpet sounded, sending an embarrassed

flush over her skin as if she'd been caught doing something highly inappropriate.

A soft chuckle slipped across her senses. Apparently she had been caught. Her blush went darker, but it didn't seem to faze him. Instead, his mouth trailed across her blazing skin, morphing the heat into something completely different.

Suddenly, another trio of women appeared before them. They were clothed in something that looked remarkably like the costume she wore. Flimsy strips of material wound around their bodies, covering in strategic places while leaving most of their skin exposed. Leaves and flowers twined in their long hair, trailing down their backs. They bounced and leaped, throwing flowers and petals into the air as they went and letting them drift in a trail across the floor behind them.

Suddenly a gust of cold air slipped up Alyssa's dress. A shiver raced down her spine, but before she could complain the chill was banished by his fingers slipping over her wet sex.

She gasped. And bucked. And then froze in place, as if she held perfectly still no one would notice what was happening.

Shifting, she tried to pull her hips away, but he held her fast.

"So hot and wet," he groaned against her shoulder. "Do you know how sexy that is? How much your uninhibited reaction makes me crazy with wanting to taste and touch?"

At his words, her body clenched, wanting him buried inside. But he didn't give her that. Instead, he played and teased. His talented fingers stroked the entrance to her body, sending a shower of sparks shooting through her.

She couldn't quite muffle the moan straining to break free, not when he was giving her the barest hint of what she craved.

"What has you more turned on, hmm, Alyssa? Knowing that at any moment someone could walk down here and see us? Or maybe get bored with the procession and look up here to notice your face flush with passion?"

Slowly, his thumb began to circle her clit, not quite touching, but coming mind-numbingly close before slipping away again. She throbbed. Her heartbeat lodged right there behind the bundle of nerves begging for relief. Her lungs burned, unable to get enough oxygen to control the need.

His fingers finally dipped inside, drawing a ragged breath from her even as he unerringly found that secret spot that made her knees go weak. Her body sagged against the railing as he alternated between teasing and stroking deep.

It was an assault on her senses. She could feel the explosion building, tension winding through her tighter and tighter like a rubber band being pulled back in preparation for the cracking snap.

"Or maybe watching the couples on the dais caressing each other in full sight of everyone. Doing something wicked."

Alyssa shook her head, unable to find the words to answer him. Although she wasn't sure she knew.

"Why did you take your clothes off for me? Most women would have been shocked and indignant. They would have scrambled to cover up, not continued to let me see more."

Again, she shook her head. And his delicious torture

stopped. Alyssa whimpered, her hands tightening around the railing.

She felt his rumbling denial more than heard it. His mouth brushed softly against the nape of her neck as he coaxed, "Answer my question."

Desperation pushed her to find the power of speech. "I don't…I don't know."

"I think you do."

Besieged by sensation and drowning in a relentless craving, somehow words began to pour from her. If she hadn't been mindless she never would have let them free, which he no doubt already knew.

"I don't think I would have done it if anyone else had been standing out there. It was the way you were watching me. Like you'd starve without another glimpse. Like there was nothing in the world you wanted, needed, more than me. I've never felt that…"

"Desired?"

"Visible. Wanted."

Behind her, he let out a sound, a cross between a sigh and a groan. She thought he liked her answer, until his fingers disappeared completely.

She cried out, couldn't stop the protest from bursting through her parted lips, no matter who might hear.

Below, a litter appeared, supported by four of the biggest men she'd ever seen. A rousing cheer went up in the ballroom, drowning out everything except the rending tear of a condom package behind her.

Alyssa whimpered with relief. And then had a moment of panic as the reality of what they were doing hit her. Was she really going to let him take her from behind on the balcony in the middle of a ball? His hands spanned her waist, drawing her close. She could feel the imprint of each of his fingers on her skin, long lines that seemed to brand her. He hesitated, poised behind her, muscles coiled with the same tension driving her.

Bending close, he whispered, "Tell me you want this, Alyssa."

And she realized he was giving her a chance to change her mind.

That wasn't going to happen. "Yes, I want this. Please."

Apparently, that was all the assurance he needed. Seconds later he was surging deep and she no longer gave a damn about anything but the way he filled her.

He paused, letting her body adjust to him. Her internal muscles tensed and then relaxed, letting him slip in the last few inches.

She was drowning, in sensation and the excitement of possible discovery. But his strong arms and unrelenting hold anchored her in place. She needed an anchor, desperately, otherwise she was afraid she'd go flying and never be able to find the ground again.

The hot weight of his palm smoothed down her spine, sending a ripple in its wake. She arched, grinding her hips tighter into him. His fingers curled around her waist.

And then he started moving. Easy, deliberate strokes. All the way out and then all the way in. The material of her dress worked between her folds, rubbing relentlessly against her swollen clit.

"When the litter reaches the dais, Bacchus will alight and the true revelry will begin. The crowd who've been held captive by the entertainment will drift away. No doubt some will look up. Maybe come upstairs for a quiet spot of their own. How long do you think it'll be before we're discovered?"

Alyssa's eyes widened. The litter was already halfway

across the room. Her heart thumped erratically. Adrenaline shot into her system, mixing with the already thrumming arousal, whipping it all into a heady concoction.

Her body quivered, and buried deep inside her he could no doubt feel the reaction his words caused.

"Do you want an audience, Alyssa? Or is just the threat of discovery what intrigues you?"

"No, please, no audience," she begged. It was one thing to put herself on display for him, completely another to have strangers witness that kind of vulnerability. Stripping, she'd had control. But she knew the orgasm building deep inside her was going to rip her apart, send her into oblivion and leave her completely defenseless.

She didn't want to share that with anyone but him. Didn't trust anyone except him to protect and shelter her in those moments.

His only answer was the increased tempo of his thrusts, but she knew he understood. At the moment they were completely alone, cocooned at the end of the balcony in shadows and at least twenty feet away from the nearest partygoer. Below, the music and revelry shielded any sounds she might not be able to smother.

He'd given her the semblance of danger without much actual potential of discovery. He'd fulfilled her fantasies in a way that let her have them without smashing the fears that still coiled tight around her soul.

Gratitude swelled inside her just as surely as the pleasure building to fever pitch. He drove into her over and over again. Alyssa met his pace, her own hips surging back and forth, racing headlong for the relief he promised.

The litter stopped before the dais. A man descended,

a pleasantly wicked smile on his face and a laurel wreath crowning his head.

Oh, God, it was almost over.

Reaching around, he found her clit and rubbed. And her body exploded.

The orgasm tore through her, leaving her blind and breathless. She had enough mental capacity to bite down on her lip to keep from crying out, but her throat strained against the need to give voice to her pleasure. It rolled through her in waves, one after the other, going on and on as he continued to draw it out as long as possible.

Spent, every muscle in her body went lax. Without the railing and his grip on her hips she probably would have slithered down into a puddle at his feet.

Bacchus raised his hands and delivered a welcome Alyssa didn't hear. His eyes swept the crowd and then traveled up, up, up. She could have sworn his gaze snagged on hers and held.

But she was too boneless to care anymore.

"Gorgeous," her masked stranger breathed, right before he gathered her into his arms and spun them both around.

He moved them through the shadows to the back of the balcony and a door tucked into the wall. She heard the swoosh and click behind them, but couldn't really find enough energy to focus and figure out where they were. Not yet.

Something hard and chilled pressed against her back. A wall. His heat bracketed her front. Fingers dug into the soft globes of her ass, boosting her up.

"I need you. Now," he growled.

Alyssa wrapped her legs around his hips, opening herself up and silently giving him permission to do whatever he wanted. Somewhere in the corner of her mind registering the tremble of her thighs.

In one long surge, he filled her again, drawing a gasp and making her eyes roll back into her head. How could that feel so good so soon?

Still breathless from her last release, she wanted him all over again. Wanted the frenzy and emotion and relief.

Wanted to let go of everything except the way he made her feel.

Wanted to look deep in his eyes when he finally let go.

Wanted to see his face.

8

BLINDING NEED THROBBED through him. Watching Alyssa Vaughn let go was the sexiest thing he'd ever seen. Possibly because something told him she didn't do it very often. She was so uptight and controlled. Knowing *he* could make everything else fade away for her was heady stuff. The kind of craving no rehab could cure.

And he wanted more. Not just his own release, but hers, again and again and again.

Even now he could feel her tight muscles contracting around him in a seductive motion that begged him just to let go. But he wasn't ready for this to be over yet.

If this moment was all he'd ever get of Alyssa, he was determined to take his time and get his fill.

Which could take all night.

Wrapping her wrists together in his hand, he pushed them against the wall above her head. Bending down, he found the thrumming beat of her pulse and sucked, hard. She moaned deep in her throat, the back of her head dropping with a soft thud.

Her body quivered, already begging him for more.

"Greedy little thing, aren't you?" he whispered against

her skin. The scent of her, strawberries, sunlight and the sharp tang of sex, filled his lungs. God, he wanted more. If either of them was greedy, it was him.

"Not usually," she answered breathlessly.

Beckett chuckled. She probably had no idea what she'd just admitted to him with those two innocent words. There was relief in knowing he wasn't the only one overpowered by whatever was happening between them.

Not even knowing she was going to be pissed with him when she realized the truth could make him walk away.

"Not complaining," he assured her, rocking his hips against her in short little bursts.

Her breath caught in her throat and her thighs squeezed around his waist. Her hips moved, writhing against him, trying to get more.

He was already skating the edge, and it wasn't going to take much for him to explode. Beckett wanted her with him when he did, needed the connection of sharing that moment.

Using the weight of his body, he pressed her against the wall. His free hand roamed over her body; the one and only thing wrong with the moment was that she wasn't completely naked. But he used that as well, dragging the soft layers of her dress across her skin, letting his fingers sneak beneath the barrier to touch here and there.

Her muscles jumped and clenched. His fingers tweaked her peaked nipples and her sex clamped hard around his cock. Beckett hissed, unable to stop his reaction to the feel of her already tight body gripping him harder.

It hadn't taken her long to realize she was far from helpless, even if he did have her pinned against the wall. She tortured him, gripping and releasing, gripping and releasing. Wiggling in the tiniest circles. Reaching between them, he found the already sensitive bundle of nerves buried between the wet lips of her sex. His fingertip grazed against her and it was her turn to hiss with pleasure.

She forgot her little game and simply gave herself up to the sensations he was drawing from her body. It was gratifying and sexy and made him feel powerfully masculine.

He ached. Throbbed. He wanted to move harder, deeper—*needed it* —but not yet. When he felt the first ripples deep inside her body, he finally let himself go.

Pulling back, he relished her whimper of protest even as he surged back, burying deep. His eyelids fluttered, fighting the urge to close, to let him lose himself completely in the feel of her.

Her heels dug into his ass. His pants, the only things protecting his skin from the sharp points of her silver sandals, were still bunched around his hips.

How could he be fully clothed and still feel completely exposed?

Beckett kept up a relentless rhythm, driving them both desperately to the edge of reason. He heard voices somewhere in the back of his mind but knew that in this secluded little closet they were safe from prying eyes.

Small gasps and keening whimpers slipped through her open lips every time he moved inside her. Her fingers curled down, gripping the hard hand holding her wrists. He understood the need to find something solid to cling to in the middle of the building storm.

"Oh…oh…oh," she cried. "Please…please…"

He could give her what she needed. And suddenly he

wanted more than anything to give her everything she ever needed, not just this single moment of relief.

Buried deep inside her, he knew the second her orgasm hit. The way her muscles constricted and then rippled, wave after wave coaxing him down into his own release.

A knowing, satisfied smile curled his lips. Finally. *Finally.*

Her body stilled, but he was too far gone to consider it anything but bliss mingled with physical release and exhaustion.

The orgasm exploded out of him, almost taking him by surprise. His vision blurred. His hand clenched tight around Alyssa's wrists. Afraid he was hurting her, somehow he found the brain power to let her go.

He shook, every muscle in his body given up to the release he'd found with her. Pleasure. Depth. Something profound that he'd never experienced in his life.

He'd had plenty of sex—seventeen years of good, bad, quick and dirty. But nothing like this.

He was so absorbed in the experience, he wasn't paying attention. Until it was too late.

One moment he was lost in the best orgasm he'd ever experienced. The next, pain shot through his scalp as she yanked several strands of hair along with the string holding his mask in place.

Pressed tightly together, while he was still buried inside her hot, wet channel, Beckett couldn't have gotten a closer view of her reaction. It was something he'd never forget. Watching the languid radiance morph into shock, hurt and then anger.

Alyssa's expression, open and exposed just moments before, shut down completely.

Panic hit him square in the chest.

"What the hell," she growled in a low, soft voice.

He would have preferred it if she'd screamed. Lost her head. The banked and controlled fury scared him.

"Alyssa," he warned, scrambling for words that might cut off the outburst he knew was coming.

"Beckett," she snarled. "Let me go."

Beneath him, her hips bucked. Her hands scrabbled against his shoulders trying to find enough purchase to shove him away. Instead of doing what she wanted, he pushed his hips harder against her, locking her in place.

Her swollen lips parted, but he cut off her diatribe before it could start. "Sweetheart, you keep moving like that and you're going to get round three."

He flexed his hips to prove to her just what effect she was having on him. She went unnaturally still. Her only movement was the furious pounding of her pulse at the base of her throat. For a few delirious moments he thought about sucking on the spot.

Sanity returned before he could make the mistake. Shaking his head, he dragged his gaze up to her glittery, glowing eyes. Wanting the same unfettered access to her, Beckett reached up and gently pulled the mask from her face.

Her mouth tightened into a hard line, but she didn't stop him.

Although that movement seemed to spur her out of her frozen trance. One leg slid from around his waist, and her heel hit the floor with a thud. But she couldn't release the other, not with his body holding her hips spread wide and his cock still buried deep inside.

"Let me go," she tried again, her voice carrying the whip of authority. But he wasn't the kind of man used to taking orders.

"I'll let you go on one condition."

"Yes," she countered too quickly.

A smile played at the corners of his lips. Logically, he realized that probably wasn't smart, but he couldn't have stopped the reaction for anything. Not even knowing it was going to dig his hole that much deeper.

He did like a challenge.

Alyssa's eyes narrowed dangerously.

"You might not want to agree until you hear what the condition is."

"Whatever it is, it's got to be better than being pinned against the wall with your cock inside me."

Beckett laughed. Surprise shot across Alyssa's face before she buried the reaction.

"What is so funny?"

"You weren't complaining five minutes ago." He leaned closer, letting the warmth of his words spread across her skin. "Admit it, you wanted me, Alyssa. It's all you've been thinking about since the night I stood on that balcony and watched you. God knows, it's all I've been able to think about."

A shiver rocked her, and her sex clenched tight around his half-hard cock, betraying her and wiping any thought of humor straight from his brain.

As if realizing just how vulnerable their position left her, Alyssa started bucking again. "Let me go," she ground out, loud enough that the low murmur of voices close to them went silent.

"Lower your voice, Alyssa. You're upset. I get it and don't blame you. We need to talk and that's what I've been trying to get you to calm down enough to do. But don't think I'm going to let you make a scene, especially now that both of us are unmasked."

She opened her mouth and he could see from the spark in her eyes it wasn't to be accommodating. Cutting off her outburst, Beckett shoved his face close and stared into her eyes.

"I'm doing what I promised, Alyssa, trying to protect you. Don't do something in the heat of the moment that you'll regret later."

The blazing flames in her eyes cooled slightly. She gave him a single, jerky nod but murmured, "Too late."

For some reason her words punched straight through his gut. The pain of them tearing at him.

SHE WAS AN IDIOT. How could she have missed that Beckett Kayne was her masked stranger?

Had he been playing her the entire time? Gone to that balcony for the express purpose of spying on her?

Humiliation suffused her. The emotion wasn't helped by the precarious position she currently found herself in. Pressed to the wall, a crowded ballroom right outside and Beckett still buried deep.

Her body throbbed from the aftereffects of the orgasms he'd just given her. Amazing orgasms. The kind she'd thought were more fantasy than reality. Even now, her traitorous body begged her to forget everything and let him give her another.

The evidence of just how unbelievably talented he was slicked her inner thighs. Her internal muscles ached, from use and the need currently climbing higher and higher. Having him pressed full length against her wasn't the best way to keep her head clear.

So, first things first, she had to get him to let her go. Whatever she had to agree to in order to make that happen was worth the price.

Either that or she was going to humiliate herself even further by begging him to take her again. And that was something she'd never forgive herself for.

"If you promise not to run the minute I set you down, I'll let you go."

He stared at her, those stormy blue eyes darker than normal as he waited for her answer. Slowly, she nodded. But he didn't move. Instead, his eyes roamed her face, no doubt looking for some sign she was lying to him.

But she wasn't even certain herself what she would do when he let her go.

Apparently deciding it was safe, Beckett pulled his hips back, disengaging from her body.

She bit back a hiss, not from pain, but from the spike of pleasure as his length slid against her swollen sex.

Something hot flared deep in his eyes, but other than that he didn't react. It bothered her that he knew, though, *knew* the way she responded to him even if she didn't want to.

That knowledge gave him power. Power she didn't think he'd hesitate to use against her if he could.

Pulling a soft handkerchief from the pocket of his pants, Beckett stared straight into her eyes as he bent down and swiped it across the smooth expanse of her inner thighs.

This time she couldn't stop the hiss. He was gentle. Too gentle. She almost would have preferred him to be rough and perfunctory. But he wasn't. He was thorough in taking care of her.

Just as he'd been last night.

Conflicting emotions twisted through her. She wanted to hate him…but she couldn't. It would have been easier if she could keep her low opinion of him, the memory of him staring down at her years before, a mixture of horror and resignation filling his eyes just before he walked away leaving her panting, unfulfilled and embarrassed.

But that's certainly not how he was looking at her now.

Somehow, in that moment, through the expression in his gaze, Beckett Kayne and her masked stranger morphed together, his stormy blue-gray eyes devouring her as if she was the only thing worth living for.

The impact of his scrutiny had her chest tightening, need and denial and craving all mixing together.

His meticulous care made her feel…protected. Cherished. Wanted. Just as she'd felt when he'd stared at her from the shadows of that balcony.

She didn't want to feel that way with this man.

He straightened her dress, making sure everything was covered before stepping away.

Once the wall of his body was gone she was suddenly cold. The flush of embarrassment faded from her skin.

Silently, she watched him redo his fly and stuff the used condom in his pocket. Only when they were both back to rights did he put more space between them.

He gave her the breathing room she desperately needed. She didn't want to be grateful for his consideration, but she was.

In an attempt to dredge up the anger that had been blazing through her not five minutes ago, she said, "You must have been dying of laughter. Standing on that balcony, staring at me, knowing what an ass I was making of myself. Did you come there to spy on me?"

Beckett's mouth compressed into a hard slant. "No. I had no idea who you were until I walked into that boardroom." He ran a hand through the dark strands of his hair, sending them into disarray. It was the first outward sign that this was affecting him as much as it was her.

For some reason that settled her thumping nerves a little.

"I didn't want to be at the party in the first place. I walked over to the end of the balcony for a few minutes of peace."

He'd gotten a hell of a lot more than that.

Needing respite from the emotions churning through her, Alyssa screwed her eyes shut. She didn't realize he'd moved until the soft stroke of his fingers over her cheek jolted her out of her mental tailspin.

"I didn't set out to use you, Alyssa. I already wanted you. The moment I walked into that room and saw you sitting there, your beautiful body covered up once more… it was too late. I was hooked. Couldn't look away."

A sound wheezed out of her lungs, half laugh, half disbelief.

"This." He moved a hand between them. "Whatever's happening between us has nothing to do with business."

"Yeah, right. Beckett, you sat across that conference table and kept your mouth shut. You lied to me, let me make a fool of myself."

"Is that what you're upset about? Wounded pride? Do you know how hard it was to not say anything? But I knew the minute I did you'd push your masked stranger away just as surely as you were holding me at arm's length."

"But that was my choice, Beckett. You're trying to steal my work, and if you don't think that's personal you're dead wrong."

He stalked several paces away and then came back.

His fingers tugged at his hair, the gesture pure frustration.

"I didn't want to steal your work, Alyssa. I tried to buy it, but you wouldn't let me. You left me no choice."

A harsh sound scraped through her throat. "There's always a choice, Beckett. You could have taken my no and left V&D alone."

He whirled to her, sharp strides closing the gap between them. She felt anger rolling off him in pounding waves. The flat of his palms settled against the wall inches from her head, caging her in and forcing her to really look at him. The way his eyes churned, frustration, interest and heat edged with the sharp tang of anger.

"I need that app, Alyssa. It's going to take Exposed global, make it a household name. Make us both millions of dollars."

"Is that really what you care about?" she asked quietly. "Money? Does it drive *everything* you do?"

Even she could hear the bitter edge to her own voice, but couldn't temper the reaction. She didn't want to think that of him, but…she'd be stupid to think anything else.

It was the only reason he'd been interested in her before. Maybe it was the only reason he was interested in her now. Sure, he was saying all the right things…but that didn't mean they were true.

He'd obviously been chasing that demon for years. Except he no longer *needed* to fight for that next dollar. Apparently, the man didn't know how to stop.

Nothing had changed in the twelve years between then and now.

Why did that send a barbed shaft of disappointment straight through her chest?

There had been a time in her life when money was

just…there. Something she had, didn't really understand and definitely didn't appreciate. But as she'd gotten older, it had become apparent that money was what drove Bridgett. And Bridgett drove her father.

Her stepmother hoarded wealth like a squirrel packs away nuts. Alyssa hated Bridgett's manipulation and maneuvering, poisoning her own father against her just to protect Bridgett's slice of the pie…and get more.

Especially because that's not what Alyssa had ever cared about.

Standing there, she could see the same desperate gleam in Beckett's eyes. It turned her stomach and left her panicked.

"You don't understand," he growled. "You can't possibly understand."

Alyssa shook her head, sadness curling through her belly.

Beckett's hot gaze raked across her face. "What have I ever done to you, Alyssa, that you'd dismiss me completely? Until four days ago I don't think we've ever even met."

Alyssa stared at him, her skin stinging as if he'd slapped her. Part of her had assumed he didn't remember their previous encounter. But to hear the irrefutable evidence that she was so easily forgotten and unimportant…

It hurt. More than it should. More than she wanted.

And hit way too close to home. Calling up long-suppressed memories from her childhood. Her father too busy to listen to stories of her day, but with plenty of time for Mercedes to sit on his lap and babble about ribbons or puppies or dresses. As an experiment, she'd once gone an entire week without saying a single word at the dinner table. And no one had noticed—or cared.

It had been years since she'd felt like a shadow. But with a few choice words, Beckett had managed to make her feel that way all over again.

And she hated that sickening, helpless sensation.

For a brief moment she thought about telling him. Throwing it in his face and watching his reaction. Would he be embarrassed? Horrified? Or unapologetic?

But she really didn't want to know. Because whatever his reaction was, she'd have to deal with it. And she wasn't sure what she hoped for.

"Are you going to stop this nonsense with the loan?" she asked, her words a little strangled.

Beckett's jaw tightened, his teeth grinding together. "I can't."

She tried to will back the disappointment but couldn't quite manage it. Once again, she didn't matter. At least, not more than what Beckett wanted.

Pulling at the shreds of her defenses, Alyssa found the cool shell of indifference that had protected her so often in the past. Schooling her features, she scooted away from the wall. Beckett moved to grab for her. Rather than scuffle with him for control of her own body, she stared down at the spot where his hand had landed on her arm. And waited.

After several seconds, he jerked away. His hand dropped to his side, curling into a tight fist.

Dragging her gaze up to his, she forced words through suddenly numb lips. "I can't do this, Beckett."

Then she pushed the door open and walked away.

9

HE SHOULD LET her go. It would be better if he did—for both of them. But he couldn't.

The pressure building in his chest was unbearable. Restless energy consumed him and goaded him on. He tried to convince himself it was sexual—one taste of her wasn't nearly enough. But it was more.

He wanted to…know her. Uncover the significance of the tattoo inked onto her skin and find out where that tinge of sadness lodged deep in her pale-green eyes came from.

Not that getting her alone so he could indulge in her body for hours wasn't also high on the priority list. The way she'd lost herself, become completely oblivious to everything but the two of them, had been sexy as hell.

Even as his brain told his feet to stay put, he was already halfway across the balcony after her.

As he pushed through the crowd, flashes of blue, purple and black, and the taunting glimpse of her skin kept him moving forward. He wasn't going to catch her, not with the crush of people between them, but that was okay. He knew where she was headed.

Exiting the building, he saw the car he'd hired pulling away from the curb. He signaled the valet for his own car and raced after them.

When he got to her neighborhood, he parked and wove his way on foot toward her building. He had no idea why. Maybe just to make sure she was okay. Or because the hurt that had flashed through her eyes before that infernal mask dropped over her face made apprehension twist painfully in his gut.

Something was wrong. Seriously wrong. But he couldn't put his finger on just what it was.

The logical choice was her anger that he'd hidden his identity, but something told him there was more. Her misery had come several minutes after that revelation.

This overwhelming need to protect her was more than he could ignore. He wanted to keep her safe, make sure nothing ever battered or bruised her again—including his own actions.

Which is how he found himself back in the darkness of the alley beside her apartment, looking up at the window that had sent his life spiraling out of control. He registered the soft pool of light spilling out.

Going to the metal stairs screwed into the old brick across from her apartment, Beckett climbed up to the balcony he'd stood on before. Yes, he was trespassing. Hell, he couldn't even remember the name of the man who owned the property.

What had Alyssa Vaughn done to him?

Not even that rational thought could stop the pounding of his feet against metal. Slipping back into the same shadows that had hidden him a few days earlier, Beckett settled against the railing and looked into Alyssa's bedroom once more.

Part of him was disappointed to see she'd already taken off the costume. Instead, she wore a slip of a night-gown that clung to her body in a soft column that hit just below her knees. A soft green that matched her eyes, the thing was held up by two wide straps edged in lace. It was feminine, sexy and demure all at the same time.

Exactly the kind of thing he'd envisioned her sleeping in.

Moving around the room, he watched Alyssa hang up the dress he'd given her. Filmy fabric rained down from a padded hanger. Her hands smoothed the material, as if she was reluctant to let it go.

He'd half expected to find her tossing the thing in the trash. Or burning it. The fact that she was hanging on to it gave him hope.

Before he could stop and think about what he was doing, he lifted his phone and punched in her number.

Her head jerked sideways. She paused, dropped the fabric from her hands and took several cautious steps to the dresser.

Her neck curved and stretched as she craned to see the display on her cell. He knew it would say unknown, but hoped she'd answer anyway.

Her hesitation lasted until her voice mail kicked on. Ending the call, he immediately rang again.

Alyssa's forehead wrinkled with confusion, but it was enough to make her answer.

Without waiting for her greeting, Beckett said, "Turn around."

Even across the distance between them, he could see the shudder that rocked her body. Slowly, she pivoted.

Moving out of the shadows, he let her see him. No more masks. Or lies. Or secrets.

Her pink tongue swept across her soft lips. "Why are you calling me? Why are you standing on that balcony?"

"Those questions don't have the same answer."

"So give me both."

Beckett's hand flexed around the hard edge of his phone. He wasn't sure what he'd wanted to say to her when he'd made the damn call. This was a bad idea. But now that he'd started it…

"I wanted to make sure you got home okay. It was the least I could do considering the circumstances."

"Oh, no, you don't," she said, her voice grim and determined. "You don't get to act the protective, considerate hero."

"I'm far from hero material."

"Trust me, I'm well aware of that."

Her words shouldn't have stung, but they did.

"So, why the call?"

"Because I need to understand, Alyssa. What could I possibly have done to you?"

Shaking her head, she sank to the bench at the end of her bed. Dropping her head into her hand, she rubbed at her eyes. But she didn't take the phone away from her ear.

He heard her tired sigh.

Finally, she answered. "We've met before. A long time ago."

Her words sent a spike of apprehension through his belly. Had he slept with her and not remembered? No. Not possible. He would definitely remember getting his hands on that lithe little body.

"What are you talking about?"

"Twelve years ago. At a party."

"God, you must have been an infant."

Her gaze jerked up at him, a grimace twisting her

mouth and anger flashing through her eyes. "Seventeen. Well, not quite seventeen."

Beckett sucked a hard breath through his teeth. The pale green glitter of her eyes slayed him. They held hurt, disappointment and something much sharper. The damage of betrayal.

What the hell had he done to this girl?

She looked down at the floor in front of her, and he should have felt relief at the loss of all that churning emotion focused on him. He didn't. He wanted her gaze back. Wanted that emotion. Was willing to suffer through the pressing weight of it to keep the connection.

Right now it was the only thing he had from her.

"I was furious that night. My stepmother had started some trouble with my father. Nothing new, but I was fed up, tired of taking the verbal punches. I'd just gotten a lecture about promiscuity and image." She let out a bitter laugh, the sound taking on a broken, tinny quality. "As a Vaughn, I had a reputation to uphold. My behavior was a reflection on the family, my father, stepmother and little sister. People were talking and he wouldn't have that."

Her fingers rubbed against the bridge of her nose. "If they were talking it was only because Bridgett was feeding her friends lies about me. Hell, I was a virgin, and until that night hadn't even tasted alcohol, let alone taken a hit from a joint or snorted coke.

"Hell, *you* know." Her bitter gaze cut to him from beneath her lashes. "Drugs were easy to find in our school. Lots of bored rich kids with money to burn. I could have done it, but I hadn't. Maybe I should have. It probably would've made those last few years at home easier to take. But I was too wrapped up in making my daddy proud. In winning his approval and love and attention."

A strangled sound wheezed down the line. Beckett's fingers clamped hard around the phone. He wanted to reach out and touch her. Soothe her. But he couldn't. And something told him that even if he'd been close enough to wrap her hard in his arms she wouldn't have accepted the gesture.

"When that guy put GHB in my drink, it was the first time in my life I've ever been high. How pathetic is that?"

"Not at all," Beckett assured her. "Trust me, there's a reason they call it being wasted."

She laughed, the sound broken and wrong.

"Anyway, I'd had enough that night. I was tired of playing the perfect daughter and being yelled at for things I hadn't even done. I was a hormone-laden teenager, just like the rest of my friends. I'd spent a hell of a lot of time reading about sex and love. I wanted to experience it for myself. If they were going to call me a slut, I was going to earn the title. I went to that party intent on getting drunk and screwing the first guy who caught my eye."

Slowly, her gaze rose to collide with his. He knew what she was going to say before her mouth even opened. And his stomach took a nasty, lazy roll of premonition and self-disgust.

God, he hoped he was wrong. But he didn't think he was. "Me," he breathed.

"You," she confirmed. "It didn't take much to get me drunk. A couple of beers and I was well on my way to being smashed. Then you and your friends walked in the door. Someone told me you guys had graduated several years before." Her mouth twisted into a grimace. "The lure of older guys. You were exactly the kind of man my father had been railing at me about. Wild, dangerous, definitely a bad choice for a good girl. Perfect for what I wanted."

God, he didn't even remember the specific party she was talking about, but he wasn't surprised. They were all variations on a theme. The place, season and sometimes people changed, but nothing else. Not really.

They'd all come from the same background, money, prestige and power. Even as teenagers they'd realized those things opened doors, meant transgressions would be forgiven and sins wiped clean.

He'd been straddling two worlds, no longer belonging in that one, but unable to give it up completely. Not when his friends all still wallowed in that existence.

"I knew all about you getting kicked out. Everyone did. It was the topic of conversation for months. Maybe that's one of the reasons I was drawn to you. It felt like we had something in common. We danced. I came on to you. Before I realized what was happening we were upstairs in a room by ourselves."

Closing his eyes, he dropped his head back and said, "God, please tell me I didn't do something stupid. Hurt you. Push you." Surely to God he'd remember something like that. He'd never coerced reluctant girls before, but he'd obviously been wasted beyond belief if he didn't even remember having Alyssa in his arms. Twelve years was a long time, but...

Hysterical laughter slammed into his ear. His eyes popped open, and his gaze crossed the alley and found her. Alyssa was crumpled over, an arm wrapped tight around her middle and her forehead pressed against her knees.

Beckett stood there, staring at her, helpless and lost.

His body tightened and his muscles tingled with the need to *do* something. But he had no idea what.

"Oh, God," she finally rasped out. "No. Actually, that might have been better. You barely even kissed me. I was spread out across a bed with your tongue in my ear when I whispered I was a virgin. You jerked back like I'd burned you. Stared down at me with this mixture of horror and trepidation…like I might be contagious."

Slowly, her body uncoiled from the protective, defensive position she'd folded into. Without looking at him, she collapsed back onto the bed, throwing her free arm wide and staring up at the ceiling above her.

The nightgown she'd put on crept up her thighs, showing him the creamy expanse of skin. With her knees bent, her legs swung—the bed high enough that her feet couldn't quite touch the floor. In that moment she looked exactly like the innocent girl she was telling him about.

And he wanted to go back to that night and change whatever he'd done to hurt her.

"And, you know, I might have been able to get over you just walking away from me. I mean, I was pretty used to being dismissed, ignored and unwanted by that point. What really hurt were the rumors that were circulating by Monday morning. Apparently, I wasn't worth screwing, not even to get your hands on my money." Her head lifted, green eyes finally meeting his. "And everyone knew how desperate you were to get your hands on money back then."

Beckett's mouth went dry. He should say something, but what?

"I don't remember," he finally whispered into the charged silence.

"I know," she said, her lips twisting in pain.

He didn't remember, although, he had a vague memory of Mason pointing out a pretty little girl to him and suggesting she was an awkward, shy heiress who'd probably be easy pickings.

He couldn't remember his exact response, but he was certain it had been something along the lines of "piss off." He needed money, but even he wasn't willing to stoop to that level. Especially considering his father had basically married into his first millions and then proceeded to make his mother's life hell. There was no way he'd considered that option, even for a second.

He'd wanted—needed—to earn his own way, which was exactly what he'd done.

Beckett's stomach churned. He parted his lips to say... something. Anything that would fix the past. But there was no way to do that.

"Shit!" he shouted, slamming his palm down on the smooth surface of the railing. She didn't react to his outburst at all, simply rose calmly from the bed with a lithe grace that was inherently sexy and silently called him all kinds of asshole.

"Alyssa, I'm sorry," he whispered, the quiet words blasting through the space between them.

She just shook her head. For the second time in less than a week she walked toward the window as he watched, soft light surrounding her luscious body. He couldn't tear his gaze away from her expression. The disappointment and resolve.

When she reached out to her side he knew exactly what she was going to do—shut him out again.

"Wait. Don't," he begged. "Let me in."

He meant her apartment, but the moment she looked at him, her eyes full of regret and apprehension, he realized she took the words to mean something completely different.

She swallowed and whispered, "I can't."

ALYSSA SPENT THE next two days in a fog. Her body was sore, twinging in places that forced her to remember exactly what had happened between her and Beckett on that balcony—the one at the ball and the one outside her bedroom.

She was the one who'd shut him out. It was her decision. So why did it hurt so much?

Part of her kept waiting for word that he'd decided not to call the loan due, but it never came. She was waiting for a grand, romantic gesture that was never coming.

Of course it wasn't. All her life, she'd come in second. Or third or fourth. Behind her mother's memory, her stepmother, her sister.

Why would she ever, for one moment, think Beckett would choose her? She was stupid for even entertaining the thought. They'd had sex, once.

Unfortunately, that didn't stop his silence from hurting.

The decision was no more than she'd come to expect from the hard, ruthless Beckett Kayne she'd thought she knew from so long ago. But the sensual, powerful, considerate man who'd held her as her body broke into a million tiny pieces of pleasure and then followed her home to make sure she was safe, even after she'd verbally attacked him…that man, the one she wanted desperately to be real, wouldn't have left her alone and hurting like this.

Plans were moving ahead with Vance Eaton on purchasing their tourism app. They were close to inking the deal. In fact, they had a meeting in two days to sign the paperwork. In the meantime, she'd agreed to attend a charity event so they could finish the last negotiations on friendly turf.

Tuxes, pretty dresses and flowing champagne always made business more pleasurable, anyway. The better everyone's mood, the easier this would be.

Which was why she found herself, for the second time in a week, donning killer heels. At least this time she had a bit more coverage in a strapless gold dress that skimmed her body and made her skin glow. She'd dressed up more in one week than she had in the past year. Thank God this would all be over soon.

She slipped into her practical, comfortable, late-model sedan, heading off to a plantation on the outskirts of town. If a part of her wished for a moment to have the sleek power of a car like Beckett's beneath her hands, there was nothing for it. Maybe someday she could afford that kind of impractical luxury, but right now…she didn't need the outward trappings to be happy or successful.

The huge house glowed with light as she approached. Alighting from the car, Alyssa felt nerves flutter in her belly. She pressed a hand there, trying to quell the response.

Mitch bounded down the stairs to greet her. Familiar with the frequent bouts of self-consciousness that struck her at these kinds of events, he wrapped a steadying arm around her waist. But for once she found she didn't need the support.

Sure, the nerves were still there, beneath the surface, but somewhere in the past few days she'd found a sense of strength she hadn't realized she possessed.

Or maybe she was finally getting fed up with worrying about everyone else's opinion. She was having a hard enough time keeping her own wants and needs straight. She really didn't have any energy left over to worry about anyone else.

Leaning close, she pressed an appreciative kiss to Mitch's cheek before pulling out of his embrace. Normally, she didn't like to walk into these things alone, preferring to have the shield of another person against those sharp, assessing gazes.

Tonight, for some reason, the thought of having every eye in the place trained on her didn't bother her.

Striding purposefully up the steps, she could feel Mitch's puzzled gaze trained on her back, but ignored it. Pausing at the top of the stairs, Alyssa let her gaze travel over the crush of people below her.

It was a far cry from the ball she'd attended a few nights ago. Guilt niggled at her. She hadn't told Mitch—about the ball or Beckett. She couldn't. Not yet. Not when her own thoughts were so twisted she had no idea what to say.

Slipping up beside her, Mitch leaned close and whispered into her ear, "I'm going to round up some drinks and Vance Eaton. Let's get business out of the way and celebrate."

Nodding, she let him disappear into the crowd. The benefit was for a local children's hospital. It was a charity her father and stepmother had supported for years. In fact, Alyssa hoped to God Bridgett wasn't here tonight. On top of everything else, she didn't think she could handle the inevitable emotional hit.

Most of the people here knew her as Reginald Vaughn's oldest daughter. They accepted her as one of their own, even if for most of her life she'd been followed by hushed whispers. Several people flashed her polite smiles, although none closed the gap to actually speak to her.

Just as well. She wasn't great with pointless small talk and really had nothing to say to these people.

Melting back into her default position on the edges of the action, Alyssa tried not to hunch her shoulders. There was something about these things that always made the bruised little girl she'd been resurface.

Maybe it was the endless lectures that had preceded any appearance at a public event. Or the weight of worrying about every move she made and every word out of her mouth and whether or not her father would approve.

Ten minutes in, her body was strung tight with tension and the nape of her neck prickling with a warning that made her want to flee.

Out of nowhere, a heavy arm slipped around her waist, heat suffusing her side. Her body responded immediately, coming alive in a burst of awareness that left her skin tingling.

Brushing her with a tight smile, Beckett bent close and whispered into her ear, "I don't like seeing another man touch you."

"You don't have the right to care," she countered.

"Didn't say I did. Just that it bothers me."

It shouldn't matter, either that he cared or that he realized he had no claim on her. But it did. Mainly because her rebellious body said he most certainly did have a claim, one he'd staked very thoroughly.

Urging her forward, Beckett propelled her onto the dance floor, spinning her into his arms until they were chest to chest. They floated together, Alyssa powerless to do more than follow his lead unless she wanted to make a scene. And the last thing she *ever* wanted to do at these things was make a scene. She'd eat glass before that happened.

This wasn't the kind of party that featured top-forty hits or bumping and grinding. The couples gracing the floor were more likely to waltz or, if they wanted to get a little wild, tango.

Beckett tugged on her body, tucking her deep into him. His lips brushed her cheek as he whispered, "Relax. I'm not going to do anything you don't want."

That did little to settle her nerves. In fact, it stoked them higher, because they both knew there was little her eager body would refuse to let him do, even in the middle of a crowded ballroom.

As if sensing the direction of her thoughts, he put more space between them. Staring at her with those stormy blue eyes, he asked, "You and Dornigan have a thing?"

Alyssa's mouth tightened. Her gaze darted away. She wanted to ignore the arrogant question but found herself answering anyway. "No."

"Never?"

"Never. He's my best friend. My family. My only family, really."

"What about your sister and stepmother?"

Alyssa's eyes jerked back to his. She held his gaze and reiterated with slow, deliberate words. "Like I said, my only family."

Beckett nodded, but didn't ask any more questions. She was used to people dismissing her complicated response to her family. Most just assumed she came from money and therefore had everything she could ever want. Beckett Kayne knew better.

The song ended. Instead of leading her into another,

he settled his palm in the small of her back and propelled her to the tables circling the floor.

A few paces in she realized why. Mitch stood beside two men, Vance Eaton and an older man she'd never met before. Eaton was in his late forties. He'd made his fortune by acquiring troubled businesses and making them better. The other man, silver haired and distinguished, appeared to be in his mid-sixties.

She ignored Mitch's pointed glance at Beckett, held out her hand to Eaton and bestowed a beautiful smile on him. "I'm so glad we could conduct business here, Mr. Eaton. Much more enjoyable than a conference room."

Engulfing her hand with his, the other man matched her smile. "Vance. Please, call me Vance. I never turn down the opportunity to watch a beautiful woman sweep across the dance floor. I hope you'll give me the chance to show you a step or two."

Alyssa inclined her head. Beckett's arm, which she'd forgotten was looped around her waist, tightened. She'd thought it was because Eaton was flirting, until she glanced back at him and noticed his hard gaze trained on the older gentleman.

"Dad," he said, spitting out the single word in a way that sounded more like a curse than a greeting.

"Beckett," the man said, a challenging smirk tugging at his lips.

The older man's eyes dragged across the arm holding Alyssa close. Blue eyes, the same turbulent shade as his son's, met hers, but they were cold, calculating and…shrewd. The similarities ended with color. Alyssa fought down a shiver.

Whenever Beckett looked at her, her body warmed through with an immediate reaction that irked her most of the time because she couldn't control it. She always fought the sensation that he could see far beyond what she actually wanted him to notice.

The only thing Mr. Kayne's perusal made her want to do was turn and run. Her body stiffened. Beckett's fingers tightened around her hip, pulling her just an inch farther into the shelter of his embrace.

"I was under the impression that Beckett was attempting to forcibly take your company."

Mr. Kayne's focus shifted back to his son. Pressed against Beckett, Alyssa could feel the strain stretching him tight. For some reason, she wanted to take the focus away from him…to give him whatever relief she could manage.

Before she could follow through on the thought, Mr. Kayne's mouth twisted into an unpleasant sneer. "Nice to see you've finally wised up. Why settle for one measly app when you can literally screw her out of her entire company?"

Alyssa gasped. Mitch's eyebrows slammed together in an unpleasant frown.

And beside her, Beckett growled low in his throat. The vibrations of the sound echoed through Alyssa and for some reason started an avalanche of reaction cascading through her body—awareness, arousal and elation at his protective, primal response.

Not that she needed it.

"Excuse me?" she asked, her voice tight with warning. She strained forward against Beckett's hold, glaring at the man who'd just insulted her. Gone were the nerves from earlier, vanished beneath the indignation slamming through her.

"Who the hell do you think you are? You don't know

me from Adam and I resent your insinuation that I'm only worth what's between my legs. Or that I can be bought with a few well-placed orgasms."

Mitch's eyes widened. Eaton's mouth twitched. Mr. Kayne just laughed, the sound acrid and harsh.

"Well, she certainly is spirited, isn't she?" The man's eyes raked down her body in a way that made her skin crawl.

Reaching out, he slapped a hand across his son's shoulders. "Lucky bastard. The spunky ones are always good in bed."

Every muscle in Beckett's body coiled for attack. Alyssa could feel the impending doom gathering to explode. As much as she wanted to lash out at the man herself, some instinct told her the greater threat right now came from Beckett.

She really didn't want him losing his head over her. Not now. Not in the middle of a party with New Orleans's upper crust society watching the melee and just waiting to spread their names with the latest gossip.

Leaning back into his body, Alyssa positioned herself as a shield between the two men. Beckett's tight fingers tried to move her out of the way, but she dug the sharp points of her heels into the floor and stood her ground.

"Don't," she whispered, running her fingers down his arm.

Alyssa couldn't tell if Kayne was oblivious to the tight hold his son had on his control, or if he was purposely trying to provoke a response when he blithely continued. "If what happened at the Bacchanalia is any indication, you could do worse than this little firecracker. Hardly the frigid, uptight bitch your mother turned out to be. This one has just enough tramp beneath the polish to make things interesting."

Alyssa's cheeks heated with a blinding combination of anger and embarrassment. She was intimately familiar with humiliation. But no one, not even the stepmother who'd made it her mission in life to insult Alyssa with sharp, veiled barbs, had ever made her feel so mortified.

The problem was, she didn't want to feel ashamed about what she'd done with Beckett. Not when he'd made her feel alive and treasured, something she'd rarely experienced in her life.

Alyssa met the older Kayne's cold gaze. He was waiting for her reaction. He wanted her to fall apart or lash out or…something.

Which is exactly why she wasn't going to give it to him. Instead, she said in a low, calm, almost-bored voice, "Right now, I'm the only thing preventing Beckett from decking you so hard your ass breaks through the floorboards when you fall backward. I suggest you keep any more observations about my personality to yourself or I'm going to forget why holding him back is important, Mr. Kayne."

He laughed. Actually laughed in the face of her disdain and the three men now wearing murderous expressions. Mitch and Eaton flanked her and Beckett. And although she didn't necessarily need the show of solidarity, she appreciated it nonetheless.

"Would appear you have some competition, son. Although, we both know there's nothing you like more than a challenge." Mr. Kayne's chilling blue eyes found hers again. "When you get tired of playing with the little boys, come find me. I can offer you so much more than Beckett."

Alyssa's blood went cold. Beckett's fingers tightened, rubbing the bones of her wrist together painfully. Covering their joined hands with her own, she stroked her fingers down his—not just a silent request for him to let up, but in reassurance she'd been far from ready to offer five minutes ago.

For some reason, this little spectacle changed everything. It was no secret that Beckett's father was an asshole. He'd thrown Beckett out when he was eighteen, cutting him off from everything without so much as a second thought.

Not that it had stopped him. Beckett was smart and determined. He'd become successful despite the things his father had done.

If there was one thing Alyssa understood, it was dealing with the fallout from a crappy father-child relationship.

"I seriously doubt that, Mr. Kayne. You have no idea what Beckett gives me."

His eyes flashed dangerously. "Oh, but I do. And I have the photographs to prove it."

10

BECKETT'S BODY SEIZED. Every single muscle froze. But his mind raced.

His father wasn't bluffing. He could tell by the smug smile tugging at the man's lips. He thought he had Beckett backed into a corner.

The familiar helplessness washed through him, along with a red-hot rage. The combination dragged him right back to when he was eighteen and powerless against the painful words his father had flung as he'd yanked the life Beckett had always known out from under him.

But he wasn't that useless teenager anymore. He'd made something of himself, fought tooth and nail for every penny he now had stashed in the bank.

And his father's continued disdain wasn't his problem.

The photographs were, though. If it had simply been him, Beckett might have laughed in the man's face and dared him to do his worst. But Alyssa was involved and he'd do anything to prevent her from experiencing any more humiliation at his hands.

However, a charity ball wasn't the time or place to discuss it.

It cost Beckett quite a bit, but he ground his teeth together and prevented the litany of curse words from falling through his lips. Alyssa's calming hand on his arm was like an anchor, one he needed to keep from losing his head.

"Don't," she whispered in a low, calm voice. "That's what he wants."

Beckett knew she was right. His father was always poking and prodding to get a response. No matter how much he tried to cut the man out of his life, his father still remained Beckett's one weakness. The ghost he couldn't exorcise or ignore.

Mitch and Vance managed to pull his father away from their small group. Beckett watched the three men disappear into the crowd, his hands still clenched into hard fists.

Somehow he and Alyssa ended up in his car, heading back toward town. He drove, pouring all of his frustrations into handling the powerful machine.

Alyssa remained silent, which only made the guilt and anger build and build unchecked inside him. He waited for her outburst—and she had every right to it—but it never came.

"Dammit all to hell!" he ground out, unable to contain his frustration any longer.

Alyssa watched him, her eyes luminous in the darkness of the car. "So you think he really does have photos?"

He stole a glance at her, wishing he could give her another answer. But lying wouldn't solve anything. "Yeah. He's been a member of the society for years. I'm sure he was there. Or had someone keeping an eye on me. I'm so sorry, Alyssa."

She shrugged her beautiful bare shoulders. Her body rubbed against the soft leather seat of his car with a whooshing sound that echoed through him. He wanted to reach out and pull her into his lap, wrap her in his arms and prevent anything from touching or hurting her ever again.

But he couldn't do that. Especially since he was responsible for this latest mess. No, he hadn't taken the photographs, but he'd put her in the position to be exposed.

And it didn't matter that he'd thought the ball was protected and the balcony safe. Or that he'd shielded her body with his own to make sure she wasn't on display.

Or that she'd enjoyed the experience.

He didn't care how, but he was going to fix this.

With a sigh, Alyssa turned to look out the window. He'd almost prefer it if she yelled. This pensive woman was too close to the broken girl he'd envisioned when she opened up and shared her past with him last night.

"Where are we going?" she finally asked.

"My place."

That drew her gaze back to him. Her eyes glowed through the murky shadows, penetrating and contemplative as she studied him. He could practically see the wheels spinning and not for the first time wished he had a direct line to the thoughts running through her head. She was intelligent and intriguing. Solitary and contained, even if last night proved there was a well of passion just waiting for the right catalyst to erupt.

Knowing she didn't give that to many people made him want to stretch and preen and beat his chest…and run his fingers gently down the slope of her jaw and soft skin. It made him crazy and more than a little panicky.

His fingers gripped harder around the leather-covered

steering wheel, waiting for her to protest and demand he take her somewhere else.

But she surprised him, finally nodding her head before turning again to look at the city whizzing past them.

Her quiet acceptance should have had the anxious energy buzzing through him subsiding. Instead, the low thrum of the powerful engine rumbled up through his body, doing nothing to dispel the pressure building inside him. In fact, the vibrations seemed to ratchet it higher. By the time they pulled into the garage beneath his building, Beckett was balanced on a knife-edge—ready to devour Alyssa the moment they reached a private space.

Nestling a palm in the small of her back, Beckett guided her to the private elevator and into his penthouse apartment. Each staccato click of her heels against his floor reverberated through him like a shot.

He could have afforded a mansion with historic roots. Or one of the renovated properties in the Quarter. Neither of those options had appealed, but the clean lines, gorgeous view and simplicity of this place had spoken to him.

Outside, the lights on the bridge winked. Stars reflected off the glassy surface of the river. Soft moonlight washed over Alyssa's body. As always, Beckett was drawn to her.

Hands shoved deep into his pockets—it was either that or touch her and he wasn't sure she wanted that right now—Beckett tried to ignore the rush he felt when she brushed against him. The small sound of her sharp intake of breath ricocheted through him all the way down to his groin. He wanted to hear more of those breathy little sounds. And he wanted to hear her scream his name without the need for suppressing her response.

The air between them heated, becoming oppressive with the mugginess of their desire. It clung to him and dewed her skin like the most brutal New Orleans summer.

They stood next to each other, both trying to pull the heavy air into their struggling lungs.

Pale-green eyes collided with his in the reflection of the window. He could read the roiling energy just as surely as he knew chaotic yearning was locked deep inside his own gaze. Her sharp white teeth sank into her bottom lip, tugging it into her mouth. God, he wanted to kiss her.

As if she were reading his mind, her pretty pink lips parted. And Beckett couldn't hold himself back anymore.

Grasping her shoulders, he pulled her to him. "God, I want to see you, Alyssa. Every creamy inch of pale skin. Do you know how torturous it is to have been buried deep inside when pleasure rippled through you, sucking me down, but not to have ever seen all of you?"

Her only response was a gasp followed by a melting groan.

"I want you spread out across my bed, open and eager for every touch." He wanted nothing between them— clothing, anger, business, and especially not other people.

Tonight, Alyssa was his and his alone.

His brain warred with itself. Part of him was desperate to strip her as quickly as possible. The rest relished the idea of slowly, deliberately unveiling her body, the best, most precious gift ever. Before he could decide, Alyssa was doing it for him.

Putting her palm in the center of his chest, she pushed until he took a single step backward. Reaching around, she grasped the tab of her zipper and tugged. He watched, in the reflection of the window behind her, as a creamy triangle of skin was revealed, slowly growing bigger and bigger.

Tension released, her dress began to gape, slipping inch by excruciating inch down her body until gravity finally won. Her dress puddled on the floor at her feet, a mound of pale gold satin that perfectly matched the highlights in her hair.

The black bra and panties she wore were a temptation all their own. As far as Beckett was concerned, they covered way too much skin.

"First thing tomorrow, I'm buying you a thong."

Alyssa laughed, the sound rich and resonant. It rang through him like the vibrations of a bell.

At the end of his rope, he reached for her, but she stopped him with a single shake of her head. He had visions of that first night, of her shutting him out and leaving him aching and wanting.

But with nimble fingers, she quickly promised him that wasn't happening tonight. Snapping the front clasp open, she spread the cups of her bra wide, baring beautiful, round breasts.

The single tantalizing peek at her nipples he'd gotten before had hardly done them justice. Drawn into tight points, they had to ache with the need for relief. He felt the same urgent demand throbbing through his own body.

"Gorgeous," he whispered, bridging the gap to draw one deep into his mouth. He couldn't help himself.

Alyssa whimpered, sagging against the window at her back. A hiss slipped through her lips. Her spine arched away from the cool glass, pushing her breast harder against his tongue.

"So sweet," Beckett growled, rolling, licking, nipping

and teasing. She writhed beneath his caresses, telling him without words just how much she enjoyed the sensations he was giving her. Her fingers tunneled deep into his hair, holding tight.

He was drowning in her, certain he'd never get enough of the delicious taste, when she suddenly pushed him away.

Her elbows locked straight, she held him at arm's length as she studied him with hooded eyes. Desire, promise and need—he understood everything she didn't say but couldn't hide. Because he was as overwhelmed as she was.

Taking a step away, Alyssa hooked her fingers in the band of elastic hugging her hips. Slowly, she rolled, pushing the satin down her legs. The slip of black material fell to the floor at her feet, but the way her body had folded kept her hidden.

He wanted to pull her up and press her back into the glass so he could see all of her against the backdrop of the city he loved so much. But when she glanced at him, letting her gaze wander lazily up his body as if she couldn't get her fill of looking at him, Beckett found he couldn't move.

Holding his gaze, she pivoted, spreading her thighs wide. Beckett groaned deep in his throat. God, she was gorgeous. And he couldn't stop himself from touching. Not anymore.

REACHING OUT, ALYSSA wrapped her fingers around the waistband of Beckett's slacks, intent on undressing him as quickly as humanly possible. But he had other ideas.

Grasping her by the shoulders, he pulled her up and into his body. She collided with his hard chest. Rough material abraded her tightened nipples, pulling a shocked rasp through her parted lips.

His hot mouth was everywhere, neck, shoulders, ribs and hips. Suckling, tasting, taking. Fingers teased and tickled, pressed and aroused.

His thigh settled against her, pushing her own open wider.

Alyssa tried to get control—of him and herself—but it was no use. Not when Beckett was staring at her, his gaze lazy and intense all at once as he scraped it down her from head to toe. As if she was the only thing that mattered in the world…and he was going to take all day and night to savor her.

A fine tremble rocked Alyssa's body.

Smoothing his hands down her arms, he placed her hands, one at a time, on his shoulders before dropping to his knees in front of her. Alyssa sucked in a harsh breath, her body humming with the realization of what he intended. What she was desperate to have.

What would those talented lips—and that crooked smile—feel like against her sex? She shifted restlessly, unconsciously opening to give him what they both wanted. God, the anticipation was killing her. Was too much.

Her fingers dug into his skin. There was something about this that felt more intimate than having him stroking deep inside her. Made her feel more exposed than stripping for him on a balcony or having sex in a crowded ballroom.

Beckett Kayne was on his knees in front of her. There was a time in her life when this would have been a fantasy, one followed by her sending a well-placed knee to his nose. Now, she wanted his touch more than her next breath.

He parted her folds, slipping his fingers through the evidence of her arousal, for him. It was something she couldn't have hidden even if she'd wanted to. And she didn't. What was it about this man that made her want to reveal everything she kept coiled up and protected deep inside?

He rubbed his nose against the damp curls covering her sex, inhaling deeply. The gust of displaced air against her throbbing sex nearly drove her to the floor right beside him.

Beckett swayed. His fingers, splayed wide across her open thighs, tightened to hold them both in place. She shivered.

His mouth trailed teasing love bites up the inside of her thigh. Sliding his tongue up the V where her thigh and hip met, he murmured, "Heaven."

Teasing her, he was relentless as he built the pressure to a feverish pitch, never touching where she wanted most. Getting close to her clit and the entrance to her sex with that devilishly talented tongue before sweeping away.

Alyssa had no idea how long he kept her there, writhing, desperate and begging. She was mindless. Time was pointless. Her clit pulsed. Her sex clenched, begging to be filled—by his tongue, fingers or cock, she no longer cared.

She just needed relief.

Her fingers gripped his hair, pulling hard and urging him to give her what she needed. Finally, Beckett took mercy on her. His tongue thrust deep. Alyssa choked on her cry of gratitude. He lapped at her, laving, nipping and sucking.

The glass behind her rattled when her head and shoulders collided with it. Her legs trembled, incapable of holding her up one more moment. But she didn't fall. Beckett's strong hands spread across her hips and the solid window at her back kept her from hitting the floor.

Her body heaved with the need for oxygen, but another need trumped even that basic drive. Her head shook back and forth, mindlessly, against the windowpane. Her hips pumped, striving and searching for that one last touch that would end the agony winding tighter and tighter through her.

Alyssa whimpered, her face drawn, not with pain, but with the sharpest pleasure.

Fingers slipping through her sex, he found her clit and rubbed. She sobbed. Keeping up a maddening rhythm, thrusting tongue, teasing fingers, Beckett pushed her right to the edge.

Her thighs quivered. Her body bowed tight. And she screamed out his name, her sex rippling around the invasion even as his relentless fingers forced her to give him more.

It was like nothing she'd ever experienced before. Her existence was drawn to the smallest pinpoint, only the space she and Beckett shared. There was no one else. Nothing else. Only the harsh sounds of his panting breaths. The residual waves of pleasure sweeping through her. The way he held her, as though she was the most precious thing on the planet.

Using soft, easy strokes across her overly sensitized skin, Beckett eased her down. Pushing to his feet, he gathered her into his arms. She collapsed against him, her muscles so lax and useless there was nothing else she could do.

Her skin was slick was sweat. Her eyelids fluttered, weighted and languorous. Even in her pleasure-induced haze, her gaze drifted to Beckett's mouth, the strong column of his throat. Leaning close, she pressed her lips there, drinking in the heat and salt and tang from his skin, enjoying the silky, decadent feel of him against her tongue. She wanted more. Wanted to taste the crown of his erection, rub her tongue along the ridge of him and suck him deep.

As if sensing the direction of her thoughts, Beckett's stormy blue eyes flashed. A deep rumble rolled up from his chest, vibrating straight through her and making her ache all over again.

"I'm not through with you yet. Not by a long shot."

11

HER BODY STILL hummed with the force of the orgasm Beckett had just given her. God, the man knew how to use his mouth.

And while she was grateful for the way he could make her feel, now that her brain wasn't fuzzy with desire, she wanted the same unfettered access to his body that he'd had to hers.

Beckett wasn't the only one starving for the sight of what he'd already felt.

Pushing into a darkened room, he didn't bother to turn on any lights. That wasn't going to work for her. Her back had barely touched the bed before she was popping up again. On her knees, she stretched across to the bedside table and tugged the metal chain hanging from a lamp. Light flooded in, illuminating the entirely masculine space.

Heavy wood furniture, old and well used. Not what she'd expected. She'd taken him for a sleek and modern kind of guy, not the antiques type. Beckett Kayne was just full of surprises.

A black-and-platinum patterned spread covering the

bed. Accents in the same color palette. Abstract art on the walls. The space was somehow a hodgepodge that worked perfectly for the man standing at the end of the bed watching her.

Slowly, Alyssa crawled toward him. She stalked her prey just as surely as he'd hunted her for the past several days. Well, now they were both caught.

With deft fingers, Alyssa worked the buttons on the dress shirt he'd worn under his suit. Somewhere along the way he'd already discarded the tie and jacket. His cuffs were open. As soon as the last little disc was free Alyssa swept her hands up and over his wide shoulders, sending the material floating to the ground.

It was hard to believe, given everything they'd already done together, but this was her first real glimpse at his body. She'd felt the hard planes of him tight against her chest, the long length of his sex buried deep, but this delight to explore…

She wanted more.

Using his own word, she leaned forward and whispered, "Heaven," before trailing her tongue across his collarbone and down the smooth slope of pecs.

The soft dusting of hair scraped against her tongue, making it tingle. The salty kick of his skin flooded her taste buds, purely, intoxicatingly male.

His fingers bit into her hips, but he didn't urge her to move faster. Grazing her teeth across the tiny nub of one nipple, she delighted in his humming groan.

While her mouth played, her fingers were busy, tugging him closer. Her palm brushed down the hard length of him in one, quick, teasing stroke. It wasn't nearly enough. For either of them.

She worked quickly to free him, her hands shaking with the sudden, overwhelming need to touch and feel.

The soft whoosh of his wool slacks dropping to the floor mingled with their panting breaths. His hands tightened on her hips. Alyssa knew he was poised to take control, to push her right into that space where nothing else mattered except the feel of him moving deep inside her.

And she wanted that. But not yet.

Shoving into his boxer briefs, she wrapped her hand tight around him. By feel alone, she memorized him. The thick vein throbbing in rhythmic time to the ache centered deep inside her own body. The sleek texture of skin over rigid flesh. The tiny drop of moisture her fingers found and spread.

Sending the last barrier between them to pool at his feet, Alyssa pushed back so she could see all of him. Her whole body shook, the fine tremble having nothing to do with her own revving desire but the realization that, in this one moment, they'd gone past the point of playing games. Somehow, kneeling in front of him on his own bed made this…real. More.

That scared and excited her.

Licking her lips, Alyssa leaned back so she could see all six feet two inches of his glorious body. His skin had a natural, healthy glow. His body was covered in long, firm muscles.

Strength. That's what she saw when she looked at him.

Wanting to give something back, to make him feel as good as he'd made her feel, she sank down until her rear settled against her heels. Hands gripping his hips, she urged him forward, never taking her eyes off the prize.

Only thinking about how good he would feel and taste, she licked her parted lips. And she wasn't wrong.

Hot. Hard. Salty. She drew him in. Beneath her hands his body tensed, but she held him still. Closing her eyes, she savored the moment, tongue caressing him in a way that had him cursing softly.

Pulling back, she let her teeth scrape lightly over him. Just the hint of teasing pressure. Again and again, she went back for more. Loving the feel of him gliding against her tongue, filling her mouth.

"Alyssa, you're killing me," he breathed, his fingers tightening in her hair. She wasn't sure if he was holding her in place or fighting against tugging her away.

She wanted to drive him insane, to make him as mindless as he'd made her. But Beckett Kayne wasn't the kind of man who showed that kind of vulnerability easily. Instinctively, she knew he wouldn't let her take him there. At least not tonight.

Maybe one day…

No, that kind of thought was just going to get her hurt. She had no idea what this was, but thinking about tomorrows was just bad. They had now, and that was enough.

Caught up in the pleasure of what she was doing, she was taken off guard when Beckett surged up and wrapped his arms around her, flipping them both. One moment she was crouched on her knees, the next her back bounced against the mattress and Beckett's gorgeous body was stretched full-length against her.

Air burst from her lungs, from surprise more than physical impact. It didn't lessen the whirling sensation of losing her breath. Disoriented, it took her several moments to catch up. By the time her world righted, Beckett already had her thighs spread wide, her knees pressed up beside her hips and he was poised at her entrance, waiting.

She could feel him, right there, nudging against her swollen, throbbing sex. God, she wanted him to thrust home, but he wasn't.

Dragging her gaze up his body, Alyssa sought his eyes, a silent question filling hers.

What she saw reflected back at her stole what little breath she had left. He watched her, studied her, memorized her. The intensity of his gaze seared her straight to her soul. Patience, need, understanding...

She gave him the only response she could. "Please."

Deliberately, he slipped inside, inch by inch, until she thought she'd go mad. Her body stretched to accept him, quivered, poised and greedy for more.

Over and over, with each controlled thrust her chest would tighten with relief only to have it taken from her when he slipped back out. Delicious torture.

It wasn't enough. She wanted more. Needed him mindless and lost in the experience with her.

The pressure built, swelling higher and higher until she was afraid she might lose herself to it. Hips surged against hips. Alyssa's eyes rolled back at the unbelievable pleasure.

His invasion was startling and intimate and consuming.

"Yes," she hissed out, lifting to meet him and take more.

Her body buzzed, wild with need for what only he could give her. But he held that relief at bay, driving her straight to the breaking point and then holding her there.

Her entire body trembled. "Please, please, please," she whimpered, her head thrashing against the sharp pleasure.

"I have you," he promised, in a silky, sensual growl that only stoked the pressure building inside her higher.

His hot mouth settled over her breast, teeth tugging at her nipple. The jolt forced out a keening cry and had her internal muscles clenching tight.

It was almost enough. She could feel the orgasm, just on the edges of her consciousness, waiting to suck her in. As if sensing just how close she was, Beckett stilled. He just stopped. Buried deep inside her. She was so hyper-aware, she could feel the throb of him vibrating against her inflamed flesh.

Drawing back, Beckett surged, filling and stretching and rubbing in all the right places. Again and again, his hips pistoned against her, keeping up a quick pace.

Lacing their fingers together, he pressed her clenched knuckles deep into the bed above her head. His warm breath brushed against her skin, one more caress to her already overloaded system.

Alyssa didn't realize her eyes were closed, bursts of light breaking through the darkness threatening to over-take her, until he murmured, "Look at me."

Her eyelids popped open. Her vision filled with him. Staring deep into those roiling eyes, he was all she could see. All she wanted to experience.

His eyes were beautiful any day, but now they were full of the same need writhing hard through her, a safe place in the middle of a raging physical storm.

Joined so closely together, the pressure she'd lived with her entire life eased. The fear and rejection. Disap-pointment and loneliness. Doubts, insecurities and dread.

Beckett Kayne wanted her. Desperately. He was intent, tenacious, gorgeous and caring. A jumble of masculinity that infuriated, challenged and intrigued her. Somehow, his need for her soothed wounds she'd buried beneath a layer of feigned indifference.

They'd already been as close as two people could be, but for some reason this moment felt like more. An unspoken acknowledgement and understanding.

Before Alyssa could panic or process, her body overruled her brain. The orgasm shouldn't have surprised her, but it did. Welling up from deep inside, it engulfed every square inch. An incoherent scream scraped through her throat. Her body bowed and then convulsed, quivering with the force of her release.

Wave after wave crashed through her. She had no way of knowing how long it lasted—minutes, seconds, hours. But when she finally floated down from the high, Beckett was there, holding her. It took her several moments to realize his body was still strung tight with the inhuman grip he had on his own control.

Giving him a soft smile, Alyssa ran her still-shaking hands across his back. Her palms settled over his tight ass. Pressing, she urged him to move inside her. It was all the suggestion he needed.

She thought he was being considerate, seeing to her pleasure first before taking his own. And, no doubt, he was. But as she watched Beckett move, her gaze flitting from the point where they joined, up over his abs and chest to rest on his face, she realized it was more.

He was giving her more, holding himself in check so she could watch the same building awe, crashing pleasure and open vulnerability sweep through him just as it had consumed her.

Without thought, she accepted the gift. Wrapping her arms around him, she pulled him tighter against her chest. Against her heart. And didn't break eye contact or the bond twisting between them.

His eyelids flickered, but didn't close. His face went harsh, mouth open in a silent moan she would have loved to hear. His hands still gripping tight to hers, his arms bulged as he bore her deep into the bed.

Hips plunging, rhythm becoming erratic, he finally let go. She felt the kick of him deep inside and tightened her muscles to give him more.

A ragged groan ground through his straining throat, his body finally becoming lax with relief.

Collapsing half on and half off her, his mouth found her neck and nuzzled. A wave of goose bumps raced across her sensitive skin. Unexpectedly, her hips swiveled.

This time when he groaned, the sound was full of barely suppressed humor.

"Insatiable," he murmured.

She shifted, meaning to move out from beneath him, but his hold on her tightened, keeping her in place.

It didn't escape her notice that, despite the monumental orgasm they'd just shared, he was already hardening deep inside her.

Bending her neck, Alyssa brushed a kiss across his damp forehead, her lips curved into a soft smile. "Pot. Kettle."

Tomorrow she might regret letting her walls down, but tonight she couldn't find the strength to care.

IN SOME WORN corner of his brain Beckett realized he should probably make an attempt to put some distance between them again. But he couldn't. Not with her lithe body wrapped around his, her skin soft and pink from sleep.

It was the middle of the night. Or maybe early morning. They'd come together several times, napping and nibbling on cheese and fruit in between. He should probably let her sleep, but now that he'd finally gotten her into his bed he couldn't seem to stop wanting her.

His self-control was currently nonexistent.

That alone should have scared him. Once a loner, always a loner. He didn't let people in—especially someone like Alyssa, just as damaged and jumpy as he was. But it was a little late for regrets.

And, really, he didn't regret a damn thing. How could he, with her still wrapped around his sated body?

His mind spun, landing straight on the words his father had said last night. The more he thought about what his father had done, and the pictures he had of Alyssa, the angrier Beckett became.

He'd promised Alyssa the Bacchanalia was safe. Had pushed her past her point of comfort because he knew the edge of it would only make the experience better.

That someone—*his father*—had taken advantage of her vulnerability pissed him off.

It was his responsibility to take care of her. But he hadn't done that.

Unable to suppress a groan of frustration, Beckett started to roll away, intending to get up quietly and leave her sleeping. But a stilling hand on his arm and her sleepy voice stopped him.

"Talk to me."

Pillowing her cheek on her crossed arms, she pierced him with drowsy, peaceful eyes. Something sharp twisted in the center of his chest.

Her hair was mussed, a tangled halo of brown and blond. Her skin was pink, and across her cheek there was a crease from the sheets.

Snagging her mouth, he stole one quick kiss, murmuring, "Adorable," against her lips.

Tucking her into the shelter of his body, Beckett relished the way she snuggled into his side, shifting her head from her arms to his chest. He wasn't stupid; they had several unresolved issues they needed to discuss, but for right now, nothing else mattered.

Her fingertips played, making abstract patterns across his skin. The buzz of need was there, like the snore of a dozing giant, just waiting for something stronger to reignite the fire. And it would happen. No matter how often they came together, it was never enough.

Beckett always wanted more of her. Was afraid he always would. How bad was a craving when you could never get your fill?

But, for the moment, he was content to simply settle. His fingers tangled in her hair, swirling and tugging and letting the silky strands slide between them.

"What were you thinking about?"

A frown pulled at his mouth. Beckett's focus trained on the opposite wall, although he didn't really see it. "My father."

He regretted his candid words as he felt a shiver snake down Alyssa's spine. Digging his fingers into the nape of her neck, he massaged, hoping he could chase the cold away.

"I'm sorry, but I don't think I like your dad."

Beckett let out a soft puff of breath that sounded like a laugh but was far from humorous. "Don't worry. I'm not overly fond of the man, myself."

She waited a beat, her fingers stilling before resuming their careless stroking. "I'm sorry."

"Not your fault."

"No, but it doesn't make it hurt any less. Trust me, I know."

He heard her bitterness and hated that anything had scarred her enough to cause it. He wanted to erase the painful memories he instinctively knew were flitting through her mind. But he, better than most, recognized that nothing ever completely wiped the disappointments away.

"He could embarrass us both."

"Yes, but he'd cost himself more than he'd gain by playing that card. The Bacchanalia Ball is well respected because they rigorously protect the privacy of guests. He publicizes those photographs and he'll be blackballed. Considering he's been a member for almost thirty years, I seriously doubt he's willing to jeopardize that for a punch at me. And, really, that's what this is about. It had nothing to do with you."

Alyssa rolled her head so she could look up at him. "That's awful."

Beckett shrugged. "That's reality." He truly didn't think his father would do anything with the photographs, but it still bothered Beckett that he had them. Their very existence left Alyssa open and vulnerable. And that wasn't acceptable.

"What happened?"

"What do you mean?"

"Between you two. I mean, everyone knows he kicked you out, but were you always antagonistic or did something happen?"

Beckett let his head fall back against the pillows, and

stared up at the ceiling. It was a question without an easy answer. If anyone else had asked he would have given a quick, uncomplicated response—one more lie than truth.

But, for some reason, he wanted to explain to Alyssa. He needed her to understand.

Maybe it was the faint, dark tinge of gray outside the window, threatening to creep in and snatch away the comfortable cocoon they'd managed to build around themselves. Or the fact that never in his life had he felt this close to another person.

"He was never the kind of dad who would come home from work and throw a ball in the backyard while dinner was cooking. Hell, I could probably count on one hand the number of times my father was home before bedtime.

"He's a very driven man." Rolling his gaze down to her, Beckett tried to keep his mouth from twisting into a sneer.

Apparently, he failed miserably. Shifting, she reached out and smoothed her finger across his lips. "Like someone else I know, Mr. Relentless."

Her mouth curled into a sweetly sarcastic smile, taking some of the sting from her words. For some reason, her easy banter made his chest warm and expand.

"I'm sure I don't know what you mean."

Her eyes twinkled with barely banked mischief. Wrapping his hand around the nape of her neck, Beckett eased her up so he could cover her mouth with his. He needed her sweetness, that connection, if he was going to spill his guts.

They were both breathless when he finally let her go, and her body sank back against his. His hand still cupping her face, Beckett ran his thumb along the ridge of her cheekbone.

"My father wasn't the inspiring kind of driven. He was the single-minded-obsession kind of driven. He came from nothing. His family had money until the stock market crash. They lost everything. He was raised on stories of what they'd once had. Fairy tales that left him starry-eyed and cold.

"He seduced my mother, not because he loved her, but because he wanted to marry her money. Got her pregnant and forced her family to accept him."

A frown pulled at Beckett's brows even as he smoothed a finger over the elegant arch of Alyssa's.

"That's why it pissed you off when your friend told you I was an easy mark."

Wordlessly, he nodded. He didn't remember the specific night Alyssa had told him about, but there'd been several just like it. Mason or Campbell or one of his other friends shoving spoiled little rich girls in front of him and suggesting the easy way out of all of his problems.

And he'd been tempted. Who wouldn't have been? But he'd been bound and determined not to make the same lousy decisions as his father. He wasn't that kind of man.

Refused to be.

Out of nowhere, Alyssa bracketed his face with the warmth of her palms and pressed a soul-stealing kiss to his lips. "Thank you," she whispered.

"For what?"

"Being you."

He laughed, the sound a little more harsh than he'd intended.

Her quiet support and belief in his integrity made him…uncomfortable. He was far from a saint and over the years had made plenty of decisions that he regretted.

But the soft glow of Alyssa's steady gaze made him want to be better.

"My dad made no secret that he had affairs. I don't even know whether my mother cared, because she died before I clued in to what was happening."

Alyssa shifted, creeping higher up his body. With deliberate motions, she flung a leg over his thighs and twisted to straddle him. Her heat aligned with his sex, but she didn't move to bring them together. Instead, she simply sat there, watching him. Waiting. Offering him whatever he needed.

It had been a very long time since anyone had cared what he needed.

Gripping her hips, Beckett held her in place, relishing the comfort of her heat seeping into him.

"For the most part he ignored me. I tried not to let it bother me, but it did. My teenage years were a wild mess. I barely graduated from Collinwood. But I didn't give a damn. I was too worried about chasing whatever felt good. I figured the asshole could buy my way into whatever college I wanted to attend. It was the least he could do since the only thing he cared about was amassing more money. Might as well give me some of it if he wasn't interested in giving me anything else."

Beckett heard his own words and realized just how pathetic they must sound. But when he looked into Alyssa's eyes he didn't see any pity there. In fact, what he did see made his heart ache.

Cool, clear understanding.

"Boy, did I miscalculate, but it was probably the best mistake I've ever made. The day I turned eighteen he showed up at home in the middle of the day."

Squeezing his eyes closed, he tried to will back the

devastating memories. He hadn't thought of that day for years. Refused to waste precious time thinking about it. But now that the deluge had started...

"Stupid me, I was thrilled for about five minutes. I thought he'd come home to spend my birthday with me. I should have known, but couldn't stop myself from hoping."

A strangled sound startled him. Beckett jerked his eyes open to find Alyssa staring at him, a hand pressed over her mouth and her eyes glistening with unshed tears.

Hell, he hadn't even told her the worst of it.

For some reason, he wanted to soothe her. He was the one baring his soul and sharing one of the worst days of his life. But she was the one tearing up. For him. And he wanted to make that go away.

Because he didn't deserve her soft heart.

Sitting up, Beckett wrapped his arms around her hips and shifted her forward. Her wet heat slid against him, coating him in the evidence that sorrow wasn't the only thing she was feeling.

Her back arched and she ground harder against him, giving him permission and offering her body all at once. Beckett lifted her, settling her back down on his hard length. Her body gave, sinking around him and welcoming him in. A contented sigh slipped through her lips. Her fingers tangled in the hair at his nape, holding him close.

There was none of the frenzy from the night before. Only the easy, comfortable connection. This felt right. Alyssa felt right. Like she'd always been there, just waiting to become a part of his life.

Seated deep, Beckett simply held her to him, drawing from her strength and compassion. Her drive and determination. That buzz of energy and excitement that clung to her like an aura.

"He kicked me out. Told me I was eighteen and on my own. I wouldn't get another penny from him. I didn't have many choices. Crashed with friends for a couple weeks, but I knew I had to figure out what to do."

The tears she'd been holding back finally slipped free, rolling heartbreakingly slowly down her cheeks one by one. Leaning forward, Beckett kissed away each of the salty drops.

"After a couple weeks I used my fake ID to get a job in a club. I'd spent enough time in them by that point that it felt a little like home, which I'd desperately needed. It wasn't long before I was busting my butt and taking on more responsibility. I socked away every cent I could. Four years later, I bought the warehouse Exposed is in. It was run-down and needed a hell of a lot of work, but that meant I got it for a song. I spent every spare minute for six months fixing it up. Getting permits and a liquor license."

Beckett's gaze was unfocused, staring straight into the memories of a history he rarely revisited. "I was twenty-two and owned my own business. I thought my father would be impressed. Instead, he gave me crap for making my money in such a crass way."

"Like screwing your mother out of her inheritance wasn't even worse."

"Exactly. But his memory is conveniently short where his own humble beginnings are concerned."

There was more—plenty—that he could share, but he'd already ripped open enough wounds for one night.

Alyssa didn't need to know any more of his humiliations, especially how he'd gone to his father three years after opening Exposed, desperate for an influx of cash to keep the place afloat, and begged for a loan. His father had laughed in his face.

Just the memory of the humiliation and rage he'd felt that night was enough to have sweat dotting his skin.

But he'd survived. Gotten a loan from another source. Thrived and grown and opened more locations. Now he was poised to take Exposed global. The thought of rubbing his father's nose in his success was sweet.

Beckett's hold on Alyssa tightened. He had a beautiful, exciting woman in his life. His equal both in the bedroom and the boardroom.

Unaware of the turn his thoughts had taken, Alyssa rained soft, soothing kisses across his face. Cheeks, chin, nose and eyelids. She nibbled at his mouth before finally aligning them together and pouring every ounce of emotion into their connection.

And then the only thing he was thinking about was her.

Beckett accepted the balm of her heat, the soothing comfort of her body. He felt her reaction to the scrape of his tongue against hers. Not just the shiver that rocked her spine, but the pulsing constriction of her internal muscles clamping tight around him.

Her hips writhed against his, trying to get him deeper. Closer. Which was what he wanted, too.

Gripping her hips, Beckett coaxed her backward, staying buried inside her the entire time. Their mouths popped apart.

A frown puckered the spot right between her eyes. "Beckett, about the app—"

He cut her off before she could finish, silencing her

with a passionate kiss. She moaned in the back of her throat.

Quietly, against her mouth, he said, "No business. Not tonight. Nothing between us, Alyssa. Nothing."

12

BECKETT HADN'T WANTED to leave Alyssa alone this morning. She'd looked so peaceful…and sexy as hell. Even now, the thought of waking up with her draped across his naked body had his cock berating him for his stupidity.

But somewhere in the middle of the night, probably right around the time she'd taken him into her body and offered pleasure as a salve to his injured spirit, he'd known he couldn't just let the photographs go without confronting his father…no matter what the visit cost him.

Once the decision was made, he'd been restless and anxious to *do* it.

He could have woken her up, but they'd had a long, exhausting night and the thought of interrupting the few hours of sleep she would get hadn't sat well with him. She needed her sleep. Especially if they were going to spend every night like last night.

Visiting his childhood home always caused conflicting emotions. He had few truly good memories, the kind of joy-filled moments most kids had. Christmases, birthdays, Fourth of July barbecues…. After his mom died, those normal, happy experiences disappeared.

But there were a few soft moments attributed to this place. Fuzzy memories of his mother's lips brushing across his forehead. Rocking. Singing in a high, clear voice. Warmth and love and comfort.

However, the bad far outweighed the good.

Unfolding his body from the low-slung car, Beckett headed to the front door and rang the bell. It had been years—fourteen to be exact—since he'd walked inside without permission.

One of the staff opened the door and ushered him inside. "Mr. Kayne is expecting you."

Oh, he was certain his father was. Because it was exactly the response the other man had wanted when he'd made the audacious announcement in the middle of a high-society party—Beckett jumping at the pull of his strings. If Alyssa hadn't been involved, he would have delighted in ignoring the tug his father had given, just to see him thwarted.

But Alyssa *was* involved.

The man who'd opened the door led him down the hall to his father's office. Beckett could have found it in his sleep, but he didn't bother saying that. A moment of joyful sarcasm wasn't worth losing a man his job. And if his father found out anyone—including his own son— had been left alone to wander the house, that was exactly what would happen.

They rounded the corner to find his father standing just outside the open door to his office, his hand outstretched and enveloping another man's.

It took Beckett several moments to place the face. He'd been there last night, standing with Alyssa's business partner. Dornigan had introduced him as Vance Eaton. Beckett had gotten the impression he was a business associate of V&D. What the hell was the man doing here, with his father?

A sense of foreboding settled across Beckett's shoulders. They tightened and tingled with the need to neutralize a threat he couldn't yet see.

"Ah, Beckett. I didn't expect you to surface from your bed until at least midafternoon." His father gave him a suggestive leer that had Beckett's hands clenching into fists.

He refused to rise to the bait. Instead, he schooled his features into a cold expression, raising a single eyebrow as if to suggest the dig his father had just taken was cheap and beneath him.

The only evidence he'd hit his mark was the quick thinning of his father's lips.

Turning away from Beckett, he addressed the other man. "I'm sorry for the unpleasant circumstances that brought us together, Eaton. However, I'm certain we'll enjoy working together in the future. Fate has a way of placing people in our path just when we need them."

Beckett had years of experience interpreting his father's expressions, so he knew without a doubt the man was lying. He was laying it on thick, giving Eaton the impression money and connections had just fortuitously landed in his lap. By tomorrow, his father would most likely have his assistants screening Eaton's calls.

He'd gotten whatever he wanted from the man and was through.

Having been on the receiving end of the blindsiding dismissal, he almost felt sorry for Eaton. Especially when he remembered how the man had stepped in to defend Alyssa last night.

But it was that contradiction that kept Beckett from giving into the urge. Why was Eaton here, in his father's home? Whatever the reason, Beckett didn't like it. He didn't trust his father, which meant he couldn't trust Eaton.

Eaton offered him a brief flash of a smile as he disappeared down the hall.

Waving magnanimously at his office, his father bade him inside.

Beckett hated this room. He had memories of standing ramrod straight staring sightlessly at the front of the huge, hand-carved desk. The space was pretentious, everything inside a calculated testament to the power of the man who occupied it.

Fighting the sneer that threatened to curl his lips, Beckett didn't wait for the invitation, but slumped down into the soft leather sofa at the far end of the room. He refused to give his father the chance to take up residence behind that monstrosity of a desk.

There would be no power position for daddy dearest today.

His father's eyes crinkled at the corners, the only indication that he registered Beckett's move and didn't like it. Left with little choice, he sank into the matching leather chair cattycorner to the sofa.

Wanting to cut through the bullshit, Beckett wasted no time. "What do you want for them?"

At least his father chose not to insult him by pretending he didn't know exactly what Beckett was talking about.

"There's nothing you have that I want."

A slow, smug smile crept across Beckett's face. "We both know that's a lie, don't we?"

His father let out a sigh, the kind of sound that carried the stamp of exhaustion. Beckett wasn't buying the act.

"Did it ever occur to you that I'm trying to protect you, son?"

He didn't even hesitate. "No." The man didn't know the definition of the word, let alone the first thing about following through on that kind of concept.

"She isn't good enough for you."

A low sound rumbled from his chest, combination warning growl and scoffing laugh. "That's not what you implied last night. Then, you were praising me for screwing my way into a lucrative business deal."

"And if that's all this was, then fine. But I know you. There's more. You've been single-mindedly pursuing her for days."

Beckett curled his hands into fists. It was one thing to think his father was keeping tabs…it was another for confirmation to come out of the man's mouth.

"She's Reginald Vaughn's daughter. When he died, he barely left her a penny. A man like that doesn't, for all intents and purposes, disinherit a child for no reason."

A snort of derision slipped out. Unlike his own father, who'd cut him out without a second thought?

"She's got a reputation for wild, erratic behavior. There was even speculation several years ago that she was an addict. Not the kind of woman you want raising your children."

This time Beckett couldn't hold back the laughter. The thought of Alyssa as erratic was hilarious. And the only wild streak he'd ever seen from her was the one she shared with him. To the rest of the world, she was cool and composed.

If she was an addict he'd eat his own shoe. Running a club, he'd seen his fair share of junkies, and Alyssa Vaughn wasn't one. She'd even admitted her brush with being high a few days ago was a first.

Whatever his father had heard, it was all lies and rumors. Standing, Beckett let his actions say all he needed about the accusations. His father followed suit.

"You can't do anything with those photographs without jeopardizing your membership to the club. We both know you're not willing to do that. So whatever you think to extort from me or her, you won't be getting it."

Closing the gap between them, Beckett brought them toe-to-toe. There was a time when he'd thought his father a giant, a scary one. Now, he seemed no more than a sad, lonely man.

Leaning forward, Beckett emphasized each word. "Let me make myself clear. If you ever use those photographs to hurt Alyssa, I will spend the rest of your miserable life making you regret the decision. If you ever again speak to her, about her, or hell, be in the general vicinity of her, like you did last night, I'll make sure you eat your words…with my fist."

Spinning on his heel, Beckett didn't wait for an acknowledgement. He didn't expect one. But for some unknown reason, he paused at the door to the office. Canting his head back to look at his father, he was surprised at the flash of pain and regret in the other man's eyes.

No, he had to be wrong. His father didn't feel those emotions. Only greed and determination.

He still found himself saying, "You know nothing about her," before walking out.

"WHAT THE HELL just happened?"

Alyssa stared blankly at the phone in the center of her desk.

Vance Eaton had told them he wasn't going to be

buying their app. The room spun drunkenly, but Alyssa couldn't tear her gaze away from the damn phone.

She was deathly calm. Unnaturally calm. At least, on the outside. Inside, she was a seething mass of panic.

Those years of burying her emotions were kicking in. The familiar coping mechanisms switching on without any effort. Her shoulders straightened. Her spine stiffened. And her face went blank as she folded her hands into a perfect pose in her lap.

Mitch, on the other hand, was fiery hot. His anger raged around her, unable to penetrate the icy shield crackling and creeping in to consume her.

"What the hell happened? I left him last night and everything was fine. What changed in the past eighteen hours?"

Alyssa didn't have the answer any more than Mitch did, although it wasn't as though the knowledge would really change anything. At least, not in time to solve the bigger problem.

They'd find another city-interested buyer, eventually. But not in time to pay off the loan.

And that knowledge was really the reason her inner ice princess was resurfacing. She was going to need the cold indifference to get through what she had to do next.

The moment Eaton had uttered the words, Alyssa had known what she'd do. Hell, Mitch knew, too. Which was probably why he was currently raging. His body moved in fitful, jerky motions. His tanned skin flushed a furious red. Without warning, his fist flashed out to collide with the wall behind her desk.

Alyssa didn't even flinch. She was too mired in her own mind to react. Not now. Later.

A few moments later Alyssa was grateful for the deep

protective layers she'd already started to gather around her. But for a very different reason than she'd expected.

Her office door burst open. Beckett's father walked in, followed closely by Megan. "Idiotic man! You can't just barge in here. I don't care who you are."

Mr. Kayne ignored Megan as if she didn't exist, which didn't help soothe her ruffled feathers.

"I'm sorry, Lys." Megan threw her hands in the air and then slammed them onto her hips. "I couldn't stop him."

No, she didn't figure Megan could. Mr. Kayne was the kind of man who did exactly what he wanted and damn everyone else.

She waved away the unnecessary apology. "Not your fault."

There was no telling what Beckett's father wanted, but nothing good sprang to mind. The man had been a calculating asshole last night. And while Alyssa would have liked nothing better than to throw him out, she knew that in the long run discovering what he wanted was the more intelligent move.

She could daydream about evicting him later.

Mitch made a single, coiled move forward, the fist he'd slammed into her wall already bruised and red. Heading off disaster at the pass, she grabbed his arm and sent him a quelling look.

"Mr. Kayne, what can I do for you?"

The slow, calculating smile that tugged his mouth wide didn't come anywhere close to touching his blue-gray eyes. Deep beneath the layers of ice, her stomach flipped once in a single, sickening roll of dread. Clamping down on the reaction, Alyssa refused to let it in.

"It's what I can do for you. No doubt you've heard from Eaton by now. I'm here to offer you an alternative to the deal you were working with him. I'd like to purchase both apps from you today."

Reaching into the leather satchel she hadn't noticed at his feet, Kayne pulled out a sheaf of papers. Placing them onto her desk, he used a single fingertip to push them in her direction.

"I'm certain you'll find the terms more than agreeable. I'm prepared to double the offer Eaton made, pay two million for the social media app and settle that pesky loan problem. My bankers are ready to make the transfer within the hour."

Alyssa didn't react. Behind her, she heard Mitch shift, his shoes scraping against her thick carpet. The sharp intake of his breath. But she didn't have anything to spare for him right now. Not when her entire focus was trained on the shark smiling benignly in front of her.

The offer was generous. Too generous. Several million more than they'd anticipated receiving.

"How did you know about our deal with Eaton…and that it had dissolved? We barely hung up with the man ten minutes ago."

That malevolent show of teeth widened, reminding her of a horror-story villain. "I'm not in the habit of sharing insider secrets, but let's just say perhaps you should speak to Beckett about his early meeting this morning."

Shock and illness curdled her stomach. Bile rose in the back of her throat, burning like poison as she swallowed it back.

Had Beckett really left her alone in his bed to meet with Eaton and sabotage her deal? She hadn't been stupid enough to tell him about her plans, but considering the pieces he'd been given last night, it wouldn't be difficult for an intelligent man to put them together into a clear picture.

Was the app really that important to him? Important enough to destroy her business?

Alyssa bit back the bitter laughter stinging her nose. Of course it was. He'd already proven he was willing to be underhanded and devious to get what he wanted.

How could she have been so wrong? Or maybe she'd just been blinded by lust.

No, last night had been more. She'd felt it, deep down, the connection between them strengthening and drawing them together.

Or maybe she'd just *wanted* to feel it. There was no way that could have been one sided. Unless…was she delusional? So desperate to feel desired and treasured that she'd let a few wild nights coalesce into something that wasn't real?

Obviously, she was. Because even if his father was underhanded that didn't negate the fact that Beckett *had* snuck out on her early this morning.

In a blinding flash, Alyssa realized that even as he'd claimed her body, made her writhe and moan in ecstasy, he had every intention of continuing to screw her over and take whatever he wanted.

Damn the consequences to anyone but himself.

God, she was an idiot.

Resolve crystallized deep inside her, spreading like the cold layer of ice numbing her emotions.

He might think he had her exactly where he wanted, but Beckett Kayne was in for a surprise. She wasn't through fighting. He wasn't going to win. Shc would *not* let him crush her.

"What's the catch?" she asked, her voice brittle.

Mr. Kayne's cutting, acerbic glance scraped across her. "Let's just say you'll be dealing with me and me alone as we finalize the deal and work to bring the apps to market."

He was trying to buy her off. The man who'd abandoned his son and shoved him out into the world alone, was trying to protect him. From her.

If she wasn't so numb with misery, she might have found that funny. "That's rich, Kayne. Beckett hardly needs protection, but if he did, we both know he can take care of himself. You made sure he learned the skills he needed to do that when you threw him out on the streets."

She'd surprised him. A soft wheeze broke through his parted lips. His skin paled beneath the artificial glow of his tan.

"He told you about that?"

Some devil sitting on her shoulder urged her to get a few digs in. To call out this man's shortcomings as he'd been so willing to highlight her own.

Holding his gaze, she said, "While I was sharing his bed."

Mitch choked, dissolving into a coughing fit at her back. Without looking, she grasped the bottle of water sitting on the corner of her desk and held it behind her.

Kayne stared at her, a brief flash of vulnerability caused by her revelation slipping through. There and gone, replaced by a hard edge that had dread spinning through her belly.

No. She refused to let this man—this bully—affect her that way. She'd spent her life tiptoeing around her own family in the hopes they'd eventually want her, love her. She'd be damned if she'd cower for this man simply because she was in love with his son.

Maybe *especially* because she was in love with his son.

Even if he didn't give a damn about her and was willing to do whatever it took to rip her life apart.

"As you can guess, we're going to decline your offer, Mr. Kayne. Please don't ever come here again." Standing, Alyssa pointed to the door. "Since you managed to find your way back here unassisted, I'm certain you're capable of showing yourself out."

His jaw pulsed with barely restrained anger. With sharp movements, Kayne gathered the documents he'd spread across her desk. "You're going to regret this decision."

She seriously doubted it. "Possibly, but that's not your concern. I make it a point not to do business with ruthless assholes."

"No, you simply screw them."

Alyssa drew in a ragged breath.

"Touching though it is, your loyalty is misplaced, Ms. Vaughn. There's no room in business for heart and Beckett knows that better than anyone. You're nothing more than a plaything to my son. A novelty and a challenge. He doesn't really give a damn about you.... After all, he's still holding that little loan over your head, isn't he?"

Kayne tossed her a knowing, sympathetic glance. His pity, false though it was, cut straight to the bone. Just as he'd intended.

Alyssa tried not to let it show. She used the frigid, insulating layers of control to still her expression. But it hurt.

Because, deep down, she knew he was right.

Alyssa's knees trembled, but she hid the weakness behind her desk. Locking her body down, she forced her spine straight and stared into Kayne's expectant gaze.

The familiar walls of ice she'd used for years to isolate her from the pain formed easily—too easily. She hadn't needed them for a very long time, but today they were the only thing preventing her from collapsing in a ball of grief and self-pity.

She hated self-pity. It was an unproductive emotion, but one she apparently couldn't cure herself of.

Apparently disappointed at her lack of reaction to his harsh words, Kayne finally turned to leave. But not before getting in one last shot.

"Perhaps I was wrong about you. Maybe you are heartless enough to keep pace with Beckett."

She wasn't, but she'd had years of pretending. And she was going to use whatever means available to get herself through this—if not entirely unscathed, then as intact and untouched as possible.

13

BECKETT WALKED INTO Alyssa's apartment and stopped. He wasn't sure what he'd expected when she'd called and asked him to come over so she could cook dinner…but this wasn't it. Maybe some pasta, a quiet night together watching mindless TV while he licked her from head to toe and buried himself deep in her tight, wet core.

Not a gourmet meal served on gleaming china complete with fragrant flowers and candlelight.

He should be panicking. Probably. But he wasn't. Not with the soft golden glow flickering across her pale skin.

She stood beside the table, her fist gripped tight around the edge of a chair. That should have been his first clue something wasn't right, but he was too stunned—and turned on—to notice.

Alyssa still wore her clothes from the office, the tight skirt, pale shirt and string of pearls that she preferred.

Except, somewhere along the way she'd tossed off the heels to show her pale-pink-painted toenails. And several of the buttons of her shirt had been undone…all the way to the very edge of her bra. Tonight it was a dusty rose satin that shimmered in the dancing light.

He had to touch her.

Crossing the space between them, Beckett enveloped her in his arms and claimed her warm, lush mouth.

Breathless, he finally pulled back, whispering, "Hi," against her smooth skin.

"Hi," she said, meeting his gaze head-on. He could see the lust glistening there, recognized it because the same response was storming his body. Always did when she was close.

But there was something in her voice that had him unsettled. A…distance. Hesitation.

A sense of foreboding crawled up his spine, tightening the spot right between his shoulder blades. She was saying and doing all the right things, but this wasn't right.

Beckett pushed away, so he could study her. She stared straight into him…and showed him absolutely nothing. She was now wearing a mask, as surely as he'd been that first night. The problem was, hers had no visible strings he could sever to free her from the decorative facade.

"What's wrong?" he asked, desperation clawing at his throat.

"Nothing," she answered. Too quickly.

He curled his fingers into her shoulders. Logically he knew he was holding on too tight, but he couldn't unclench enough to let her go. She was slipping away and he had no idea why or how to stop it. She didn't even seem to notice the deep impression of his fingers into her skin.

That, more than anything, scared him. It was as if she was frozen. Hell, even her skin felt cold.

His heart thumped erratically inside his chest. Any moment he expected her to tell him this was over. Instead, she pressed closer, the warm swell of her breasts pressing hard against the tight confines of her shirt and bra to rub against his chest.

The move was deliberate. And far be it from him to complain about an empowered woman who knew what she wanted and wasn't afraid to go after it with everything she had. Any other time, he'd be thrilled to let Alyssa seduce him.

But he'd seen her blissed out with passion. He'd seen her so aroused she could barely contain the energy of her desire inside her own skin.

And she was far from that right now. Oh, her body was responding to the stimulation, her nipples hardening into tight buds where they brushed against the silky material of her bra. But her heart wasn't in it.

"Tell me," he ground out, trying to use his head to overrule the lust attempting to convince him it didn't matter, he'd take Alyssa any way he could get her.

But that wasn't true. After last night, when she'd offered him the solace of her body, he wanted more than sex and arousal. He wanted all of her—body, mind and soul.

She shook her head.

It took everything inside him, but he wrapped his fingers around her arms and shoved her away. She drew in a harsh breath, the hurt that flashed through her gaze almost enough for him to take the action back.

Until those pale-green eyes turned to glittering, cutting stones. Her mouth rolled in, her teeth grinding together.

"Drop the loan."

"What?" Beckett asked, the incredulous word blasting through his suddenly dazed lips.

"The loan. Don't call it in. Let us have the full term to pay it back."

Beckett started to tell her…he wasn't sure what. *Yes. Sure. Anything you want,* sprang to mind. But his head overruled his dick…just in time.

Snapping his mouth shut, his gaze bounced around the room, taking in the scene she'd so expertly set with an entirely different mindset than the one he'd walked in with.

Oh, it was still clearly a seduction scene. But this time, there was nothing pure about it. He could see the calculation as clearly as the twisted look of pain on her face.

His gaze raked down her body. Disappointment and anger coiled deep in his belly.

God, she'd played him.

"Beckett, please," she tried to say, but he could see the words were killing her. She nearly choked on them, forcing herself to swallow and spit them out. "Don't do this to me. To my company. I've worked hard to get V&D to this point. Don't take it all away. If you care about me at all…"

He laughed, the harsh sound scraping against his own ears. If he cared about her. He loved her, dammit.

And she was standing there, ready to use whatever advantage she had to get what she wanted. She'd called him ruthless…he could take lessons from her.

Unfortunately, she was better at writing code than she was at playing a role. It was clear from the way she'd scooted away from him, wrapping her arms around herself to block any attempt at touching her, that she didn't want to be near him. Probably never had.

He wasn't ego driven enough to think every woman he came in contact with wanted him. He'd been rejected in his life.

But Alyssa's rejection hurt worse. And what really cut him was her betrayal. He'd opened up to her, spilled his guts. The most amazing sexual and emotional experience of his life had been a lie.

"Why did you come back, Alyssa? Why did you let me take you home from that party last night? At the ball...you made it clear you never wanted me to touch you again. And one night later you're stripping yourself bare and coming all over my sheets. What changed?"

"I..." Her mouth opened and closed, like a fish caught on a line and desperate for water. Or a liar searching for a good excuse.

"Was it all about the loan?"

He wanted to hear her say no. Even as his body screamed at him to lash out or protect himself, his brain begged and pleaded for her to tell him he'd misunderstood.

But she didn't say anything, simply stared at him, her eyes clear and vacant.

God, and to think he'd been planning to do exactly what she'd just asked. Better, he already had his team of lawyers working on drawing up papers that would forgive the loan completely.

But there was no way in hell he was going to tell her that. Not now.

"I have to hand it to you, Alyssa. At least you're dedicated."

Shaking his head, Beckett tried to will back the blistering trail of bile rising up his throat.

He felt used. Betrayed. Crushed. Broken.

It had been a damn long time since he'd felt this way... fourteen years to be exact. How appropriate that just this morning his father had warned him this was all going to blow up in his face.

Clenching his hands into fists, Beckett took a step away from her. He had to leave.

"I take it that's a no," Alyssa said, her arms curling tighter around herself.

"No, Alyssa. I won't drop the loan." Bitterness twisted through his gut, a slow moving poison that threatened to rot him from the inside out. "There's no heart in business. Or pleasure."

"The only thing that matters is the bottom line," she threw at him, her beautiful mouth contorting into something ugly.

"Absolutely."

And because there was a piece of him that wanted to hurt her as much as she'd just hurt him, Beckett closed the space between them. He brushed a finger down the silky texture of her cheek and leaned close. His whispered words fell across her lips.

"I guess neither of us is good at screwing people out of money, huh?"

The ache inside her chest was a gaping wound she couldn't seem to cauterize. But she didn't have time to worry about that. Not yet. Right now, she had to save her business and prevent Beckett from winning.

She had one option left. The one she'd been avoiding from the very beginning. Bridgett.

Alyssa prided herself on the fact that, from the moment she'd moved out of her father's house, she'd never asked him or his wife for a single cent.

She'd stood on her own two feet for years. It galled her that she was in this position. And it was difficult not to blame Beckett for that, even if she and Mitch were the ones who'd taken out the loan in the first place.

His betrayal hurt. More than she wanted it to. She'd worked so hard in the past few years, keeping herself shut off and protected. One night, one bad decision, and all that work had crumbled, leaving her vulnerable.

And Beckett had swooped in to exploit the opening, using it to get everything he wanted—her and her Watch Me app.

God, she'd known better than to fall for the man. He was fierce and dangerous. It had been a walk on the wild side. A chance to explore, experiment and indulge.

Stupid, stupid, stupid.

So, now here she was, on her way out of the city to visit the one person who would delight in rubbing her nose in her misery. Bridgett's favorite phrase was "I told you so."

Alyssa winced and closed her eyes for a brief moment. The temptation to leave them closed and pretend this whole thing wasn't happening was strong. But she wasn't the kind of woman to give up.

She'd take the hit, absorb it and move on. As she always did. What was one more emotional scar?

Her cell rang, drawing her out of the miserable thoughts. Glancing down at the screen, she bit off a groan. Ignoring the call wouldn't get her anywhere though so she answered.

"Mitch."

"Megan said you weren't coming in today. What are you doing?" His tone said he'd already guessed, but was hopeful he was wrong.

"What you think. Heading to see Bridgett."

Silence greeted her words. The weight of it pressed into her through the open line.

Finally, he said, "You don't have to do this."

Mitch, better than anyone, understood just what this would cost her. He'd had the privilege of witnessing the aftermath of Bridgett's venom.

"Yes, I do."

"We'll find another way, Lys."

"What, Mitch? When? We already punted and didn't make the end zone. This is our Hail Mary. I'll be fine."

He let out a heavy sigh. "At least let me go with you. You shouldn't do this alone."

Alone was the only way she'd be able to handle it. Otherwise she wouldn't be able to maintain the cold outer shell she desperately needed to get through the next hour.

So she lied. "I'm already halfway there. No sense in turning around now." In reality, she'd barely left her place. "I'll call you when it's done."

She could sense his frustration and concern through the line, but didn't have the energy to worry over it now.

"I'd do anything to fix this, Lys."

"I know."

"GOD, YOU'RE SUCH an asshole, Kayne."

The voice echoing through his cell startled Beckett. His heart had fluttered when he'd seen V&D's number pop up on his screen. She was calling him.

Only she wasn't. Her business partner was.

It took Beckett several precious moments for his brain to switch gears and catch up to the actual conversation. Not that it really helped.

"What?"

"Do you have any idea what she's doing right now?"

"No."

"She's driving out to her stepmother to ask for a loan to pay you off."

"Oh, shit." Assuming everything she'd told him over the past few days was true and not just lies for effect, Beckett didn't need a neon sign to realize this was not good.

"Exactly," Mitch growled. "Did she tell you your asshole father paid us a visit yesterday?"

"No." She hadn't. And that bothered him, although he didn't know why. She'd been hiding things from him all along, why not that, as well?

It also pissed him off. His father had blatantly ignored the warning he'd given. The man didn't realize anything had changed between him and Alyssa.

"Well, then you're probably also unaware that he offered her an obscene amount of money for Watch Me and the app we were set to sell to Eaton until yesterday. That deal was going to be enough to pay off the loan."

What? She hadn't mentioned another deal to him. Although, if it was to clear the loan he supposed she had good reason not to.

But if, up until yesterday, she'd had an out...

Was it possible nothing that had happened between them was about gaining an advantage to use against him?

For the first time since he'd stormed out of her apartment last night a small ray of hope broke through the tormenting pain.

Beckett collapsed into his chair, relief flowing freely through him. Although, it was quickly replaced by alarm.

He'd screwed up, letting his own insecurities blind him to the possibility that he was misinterpreting the signs. He'd pushed Alyssa away twelve years ago, determined not to become his father, a man satisfied with using people to get what he wanted. And the thought that she'd callously turned the tables and done that exact thing to him had been…heartbreaking, agonizing and enraging.

But he already had a surefire way to fix the damage he'd caused. For some reason, he hadn't been able to work up the energy to contact his lawyers this morning to stop the paperwork they were drawing up.

"She turned my father down? Before or after the deal with Eaton fell through?"

A strangled sound of irritation slipped across their connection, but Beckett wouldn't apologize. He had to know.

"After."

His eyes squeezed shut with hope.

"So she really thought there was little hope for paying me back?"

"Oh, no, she's always had a surefire way to make the whole mess go away. But it's going to cost her. Majorly. So she's been putting it off as an absolute last resort. Which is why you're an asshole. If you let her go to Bridgett and beg…"

"I won't. I'm going to fix this."

Beckett didn't wait for Mitch's response before he hung up on the man. He had several more important calls to make. He didn't have enough time to cut Alyssa off at the pass *and* stop at the office. Someone was going to have to meet him with the papers.

He wanted them in hand when he caught up with her. After last night, it was entirely possible she wouldn't speak to him.

14

ALYSSA DROVE THE speed limit. It wasn't that she was overly cautious or conscientious. Her foot just didn't seem capable of holding the pedal down hard enough to push her car past that point.

Even her car was reluctant to make this trip. Although, driving slowly wouldn't prevent her from eventually arriving. And then she'd have to deal.

The closer she got to her childhood home, the thicker her protective shield became. On some level, Alyssa recognized the chill that was invading her body. But the numbness was so welcome she didn't fight it.

The long driveway came into view. A soft hitch in her throat was the only indication of the anxious flutter inside her chest. Unpleasant memories, old reactions and destructive habits stole through her.

Her shoulders automatically straightened. Her neck muscles stiffened and pain from the tension shot down her spine. A dull ache throbbed just behind her eyes.

Huge maples lined the drive at precise intervals, giving shade and blocking a view of the house from the road. One summer, until Bridgett had discovered her hiding place, those trees had been her sanctuary. She'd curled her body into the protective branches and spent hours lost in books. Worlds where good always followed bad and little girls were loved and wanted.

Guiding the car around the circular drive, Alyssa bit back a groan when she noticed a baby-blue BMW convertible parked in the drive. Of course Mercedes would be here to witness her humiliation.

God, it just kept getting better and better.

Stepping out of her sedate sedan, Alyssa closed the driver's-side door and stood there, looking up at what once had been her home.

A sprawling, three-story antebellum mansion. Somewhere along the way, the family had been forced to sell the surrounding plantation if they wanted to keep the house. A mile or so down the road, it had been turned into a tourist attraction.

Alyssa could have appreciated a home with that kind of history. And, maybe, when she was younger, she'd loved this place. But any good had long been outstripped by bad.

Now, all she could see when she looked at the dark brick and soaring columns was her stepmother. The woman's ruthless manipulation. Being summarily dismissed by her father. Abandoned by her mother. Power, money, greed. That's what this place represented for her. And insatiable hunger that couldn't be satisfied, no matter what.

In another life she'd probably feel sorry for Bridgett, but right now she was too busy trying to force herself through the next hour.

What struck her, as she stared up at the extravagant exterior, was just how similar Bridgett and Beckett had turned out to be. Both fighting tooth and nail to fill some empty void deep inside with money and possessions. Trust her to fall for a man who was the epitome of what she'd always tried to escape.

Beckett had simply been better at hiding the truth behind a convincing mask of charm and sensuality.

So why did Beckett's betrayal hurt more?

Possibly because Bridgett had made no secret about where she stood. Beckett, on the other hand, had sucked her in, convincing her she had finally found someone who wanted *her*.

At least Beckett's manipulation had never been cruel. Hell, even when he was exploiting her sexual needs and fantasies, he'd protected her.

She supposed she should be grateful for small favors. Shaking her head, Alyssa forced her thoughts away from Beckett. They wouldn't help. Not now.

Pressing her hands hard against the roof of her car, Alyssa measured the space between her and the sweeping steps up to the front door. The grimace that crossed her face was involuntary, and the last true reaction she could allow herself if she wanted to survive this encounter with any shred of dignity.

Bridgett was like a shark; the moment she scented blood in the water she'd circle, tease and then go in for the kill.

Pushing away from the car, she was halfway across the drive when an unexpected sound stalled her. Stopping, Alyssa whipped her head around to look back down the drive. A car barreled toward her, hell-bent for leather.

Self-preservation kicked in, and Alyssa stumbled backward until her butt collided with the side of her own car.

Tires squealing, Beckett's sleek Maserati slammed

into the open, circular drive, practically riding up onto the bottom edge of the steps. Blocking her path.

The low motor continued to growl as he jumped out. The door swung drunkenly behind him, completely ignored. Her body froze; surprise and something dangerously like hope stiffened her muscles.

"What are you…" she tried to ask, but Beckett cut her off. His fingers wrapped around her arms, jerked her forward and brought their bodies together. Hard and soft, he crushed her against him, burying his mouth in the hair at her temple.

All the air whooshed from her lungs, not just from the impact of his rock-solid body, but also from the emotional release of the tension she'd been holding around her like a shield.

Relief swept through her, prickling behind her eyes before she could stop it.

Pulling back, Beckett stared down into her upturned face. She expected him to kiss her. Wanted him to. And he didn't. Instead, he grasped her hand and pulled her over to his car.

He reached into the front seat and took out a sheaf of papers. Turning, he flashed them in her direction, too quickly for her to read them.

"Just so you know, I started these yesterday. That's what I was doing when I left you alone. This and confronting my father about the photographs he had."

"You weren't meeting with Eaton? Sabotaging our deal?"

The bewilderment that crossed his face was difficult to fake. "How could I? I didn't even know about it. I did see Eaton yesterday morning, leaving my father's office."

A strangled sound grated through her throat. "He told

me…" Her words trailed off, her eyes squeezing shut in a twist of anger and understanding and bitterness. "Of course that's what he'd say. Your father made me think you'd been the one to ruin the deal, but it was really him."

Beckett nodded. "Sounds like him. But that doesn't matter. Not anymore." Shoving the neat stack against her chest, Beckett wrapped her free arm around the papers so she had to hold them. "These cancel the loan in full."

"Wait. What?" Alyssa blinked.

"The loan. It's null and void. Gone."

Shaking her head, Alyssa's eyebrows slammed together. "No."

"Yes."

She should have been elated, but she wasn't. "I don't want your charity, Beckett Kayne. Or your money." She tried to shove the papers back at him, as if they were a hot potato and transferring them would save her from what they said. And meant. "I'm perfectly capable of making my business successful without handouts. I did not sleep with you for the damn loan."

Beckett's face softened. His hands slid up and down her arms, the kind of soothing caress she was desperate for.

"I didn't realize how much I needed to hear those words until just now," he said in a low, rumbling voice that rolled straight through her. "I know you didn't. Now. Last night I let my fears convince me otherwise. I've never felt this way, Alyssa. It scares the hell out of me, how vulnerable wanting you, loving you makes me. Why didn't you tell me about Eaton and my father?"

Alyssa tried to reason through everything he'd just told her in a few short words. He loved her. Wanted her. Her stomach flipped lazily—exhilaration and hope tinged with a tiny kernel of trepidation.

Beckett watched her with the same intensity she'd experienced that first night. As if he could see behind every wall she'd slammed in place to protect herself. As if he wanted to devour her and cherish her at the same time.

Accepting what he'd just said would mean trusting him. Exposing herself to him, not just physically—that was the easy part—but emotionally and mentally.

Could she survive opening up only to be slapped in the face again?

As if sensing her spiraling panic, his palm settled in the deep well at the small of her back, pressing her tight against him. He was hot and hard, mouthwatering and tempting. Even now, she wanted him. So desperately that the rest of the world began to fade away.

He was there for her, protecting her in a way no one else in her life ever had. Even when she'd thought he was rejecting her so long ago, he'd been doing it for the right reasons. To the world, Beckett Kayne might appear to be ruthless and coldhearted, but Alyssa knew differently.

With a thumb and finger on her chin, Beckett coaxed her back to him. Blue-gray eyes, clear and deep, stared down at her. God, this man had been nothing but open with her. He'd shared pieces of himself that she instinctively knew he'd never given to anyone else. And she was still hiding.

No more. Resolve spiraled inside her, warm and welcome. She was tired of masking who she was and what she wanted. Second-guessing everything she did because she was afraid of what someone might think.

She wanted Beckett Kayne in her life and was willing to fight for that—even if the person she'd be duking it out with was herself.

But she couldn't stop herself from asking, "You love me?"

A devilish smile curved his crooked lips even as his fingers trailed down her jaw, tickling across her exposed throat. "I've seen some shitty things, been through hell. So have you. We're both a little damaged, but I know a good thing when I get my hands on it, and Alyssa Vaughn, you are the best thing that's ever happened to me. Of course I love you."

A choked sound squeezed through her suddenly constricting throat. Somewhere she found the breath to whisper, "I love you, too."

Leaning up, she buried her fingers in his hair and tugged him down to her. They could discuss alternate loan terms later…and she wasn't opposed to using any methods available to get what she wanted. Beckett would take repayment. Or, at the very least, a percentage in the company.

But now they had more important things to discuss. And as always happened between them, the moment their bodies touched, passion exploded. Tongues, mouths, lips came together, devouring, destroying and worshipping all at once. She forgot everything. Where they were. Who could see. The only thing that mattered was Beckett. And the way he looked at her, as if she was the only thing in the world that mattered.

"Do I need to call the gardener for the hose?" a smooth, cultured, lazy voice drawled from above them.

Beckett pulled away, raining quick kisses across her nose, cheeks and lips as if he was reluctant to break the connection.

His eyes glowed when he looked down at her, full of happiness and devotion. Without breaking his gaze from hers, he said, "Not necessary."

"Perhaps if you moved away from my stepdaughter I might be more inclined to believe that statement."

Beckett's eyes went flinty, flicking away from her for the briefest moment before returning. *Uh-oh.*

She thought he was going to tell Bridgett to take a long walk off a short pier. Instead, he straightened, pulling her gently with him and tucking her tight against the shelter of his body.

"Alyssa Vaughn, what do you think you're doing practically prostrate with a stranger in the middle of my driveway? Anyone could see you. And while I understand that apparently doesn't bother you, it does upset me that you've brought this to my home."

A low, warning growl rumbled through Beckett's chest. Placing a hand there, she tried to calm him. "Don't."

Alyssa flicked her gaze across the woman standing at the top of the stairs above them. Her stepmother's platinum-blond hair—long since the result of a highly paid colorist—curled down over her shoulders in perfect waves. The skin on her face was tight, not just with disapproval but because she paid the best plastic surgeons to keep it that way. Her waist was thin, breasts high and perky, and any cellulite that deigned to invade her thighs had been long since sucked out.

She wore a pair of designer pants and a flowing floral top paired with sparkling diamonds and tasteful sapphires at ears, wrist and throat. Her hands were balled into fists at her hips. Over her shoulder, Alyssa could see Mercedes hovering in the background, just as perfectly coiffed as her mother.

Her mouth twisting into a fake smile, Alyssa said, "We both know this was my home long before it was yours, Bridgett, and it's about damn time I did whatever the hell I wanted here."

Air sucked hard through Bridgett's plumped and glistening lips. Small lines of disapproval feathered out from her tightened expression. Alyssa might want to get a few digs in, but she wasn't cruel enough to call attention to the signs of age not even Bridgett and her piles of money could fight.

"Is that why you came here, Alyssa? To be crude?"

That question threw her for a loop. She floundered, searching for a plausible reason for her presence since she no longer needed to beg for money.

As usual, Beckett was quick on his feet and beat her to it.

"No, I asked Alyssa to introduce me to her family. At the moment I'm regretting it." Beckett's attention traveled back to her, running lovingly over her face. "Sorry, sweetheart, I should have listened when you said she was a bitch and not worth our time."

Bridgett's gasp was like a gunshot, loud and echoing with indignation.

Alyssa had no doubt the expression on her face was closer to dumbfounded than anything else. But she couldn't stop the bubble of laughter tickling up through her chest. Especially when Beckett leered at her with a knowing, wicked smile.

Trouble. He was pure trouble.

And she loved that. Relished it. Had needed it in her life for so, so long.

Suddenly Beckett swooped her up and pressed her back against the curves of his low, powerful car. Until that moment she'd forgotten the motor still hummed. But she couldn't ignore it anymore, not with the vibrations rattling through her already revving body.

Leaning forward, just before his mouth claimed hers again, Beckett suggested in a perfectly calm voice, "If you don't want to watch me kiss your stepdaughter I suggest you leave."

Shaking her head, Alyssa grasped his ears and pulled him closer, whispering, "What am I going to do with you?" against his lush lips.

"Love me?" he suggested, a wicked glint in his eyes.

"Absolutely. One hundred percent. With everything inside me."

Behind them, the front door slammed.

Alyssa let herself slip beneath the wave of ecstasy just being near this man always produced.

After a few moments a sound broke through the fog. The quiet click of heels against brick coming down the stairs. Disengaging, Alyssa craned her neck sideways so she could see who was still there watching.

She was surprised to see Mercedes standing on the opposite side of the car. Her sister was six years younger. She had the best of her mother's beauty—what had been natural before she'd let the doctors and treatments take over—and their father's air of understated elegance.

Mercedes was gorgeous and always had been.

Alyssa's body stiffened. She wasn't certain what to expect. Growing up, they hadn't exactly been close. Bridgett had worked hard to drive a wedge between them.

"I'm glad you're happy, Alyssa," Mercedes said in a soft, hesitant voice. Her eyes, a darker green than Alyssa's, held nothing but genuine affection.

For the first time, Alyssa wondered if maybe she'd

missed out on the opportunity to know her sister simply because it had been easy to lump her together with her mother.

Disengaging, Alyssa slipped out from beneath Beckett's body and turned to face her sister. "Thanks, Mercedes. That means a lot."

The quick flash of hope was hard to miss before Mercedes dropped her eyes to the glossy black surface between them.

"I…" She hesitated, her gaze darting up for a moment, but not actually catching Alyssa's. "I'd love to get together for lunch sometime. I'm in my last year at Tulane."

How had she not known where her sister was going to college?

"I'd like that," Alyssa found herself saying, and meant it. Going on instinct, she rounded the car and pulled Mercedes into a hug. Her sister hesitated for several seconds before wrapping her arms tight around Alyssa's shoulders.

Pulling away, Mercedes slowly backed up the steps. But she was smiling, a huge, wide expression that brought light to her face.

Rolling her eyes, she said, "I better get back inside before Mother goes on a tirade," and then disappeared.

Stunned, Alyssa stared at the door for several moments after it closed behind her.

Slowly, she turned to look at Beckett. He stood there, his fists buried deep inside the pockets of his pants.

"What just happened?"

Tipping back on his heels, he grinned at her and shrugged. "Who knows? But from the outside, it looked good."

Alyssa nodded. "I think it was."

"Come here," he ordered.

She didn't hesitate to walk straight into his open, waiting arms. Pressing her face into the warm strength of his neck, she asked, "Did you really mean it?"

Burying his hand in her hair, Beckett cupped her nape, holding her close. "Every single word. I love you, Alyssa, and want to spend the rest of my days watching you, touching you, sharing our lives. We don't have to jump into anything, but that's where I want to go."

That was exactly what she wanted, too.

Reaching up, she pulled him down to her. The kiss was perfect, a blend of heat and heart. "Yes," she whispered against his lips. "No one in my life has ever made me feel the way you do, Beckett Kayne. I think I fell for you the moment I turned and caught you watching me through my window."

"How could you not?" he asked, grinning. "I know I sure as hell fell for you. One small glimpse wasn't enough. And I'm not sure a lifetime of them will be either. But I plan on finding out."

* * * * *

COMING NEXT MONTH FROM

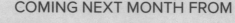

Available March 18, 2014

#791 A SEAL'S KISS
Uniformly Hot!
by Tawny Weber

What do you get when you bring together a hot navy SEAL—aka Aiden Masters—who's addicted to rules, and a sexy free spirit like Sage Taylor, who sets out to break every rule she can? Sparks!

#792 NOTHING TO HIDE
The Wrong Bed
by Isabel Sharpe

How much skimpy lingerie does it take to seduce a billionaire? Clothing designer Allie McDonald isn't sure, but her lakeside catch-and-release plan backfires when sexy Jonas Meyer hooks her instead!

#793 BREAKAWAY
Last Bachelor Standing
by Nancy Warren

Max Varo isn't about to invest in a small struggling Alaskan airline. But the heart—and body!—of this committed bachelor says otherwise when he meets sexy bush pilot Claire Lundstrom.

#794 THE MIGHTY QUINNS: MALCOLM
The Mighty Quinns
by Kate Hoffmann

As an adventure-travel guide in New Zealand, Malcolm Quinn lives for a challenge. His latest: seducing writer Amy Engalls. Amy is like climbing without a harness—exhilarating, heart-pumping...and dangerous. Because there's nothing to catch him if he falls.

YOU CAN FIND MORE INFORMATION ON UPCOMING HARLEQUIN® TITLES, FREE EXCERPTS AND MORE AT WWW.HARLEQUIN.COM.

HBCNM0314

REQUEST YOUR FREE BOOKS!
2 FREE NOVELS PLUS 2 FREE GIFTS!

HARLEQUIN®

Blaze®

red-hot reads!

YES! Please send me 2 FREE Harlequin® Blaze™ novels and my 2 FREE gifts (gifts are worth about $10). After receiving them, if I don't wish to receive any more books, I can return the shipping statement marked "cancel." If I don't cancel, I will receive 4 brand-new novels every month and be billed just $4.74 per book in the U.S. or $4.96 per book in Canada. That's a savings of at least 14% off the cover price. It's quite a bargain. Shipping and handling is just 50¢ per book in the U.S. and 75¢ per book in Canada.* I understand that accepting the 2 free books and gifts places me under no obligation to buy anything. I can always return a shipment and cancel at any time. Even if I never buy another book, the two free books and gifts are mine to keep forever.

150/350 HDN F4WC

Name _____ (PLEASE PRINT) _____

Address _____ Apt. # _____

City _____ State/Prov. _____ Zip/Postal Code _____

Signature (if under 18, a parent or guardian must sign) _____

Mail to the **Harlequin® Reader Service:**
IN U.S.A.: P.O. Box 1867, Buffalo, NY 14240-1867
IN CANADA: P.O. Box 609, Fort Erie, Ontario L2A 5X3

Want to try two free books from another line?
Call 1-800-873-8635 or visit www.ReaderService.com.

* Terms and prices subject to change without notice. Prices do not include applicable taxes. Sales tax applicable in N.Y. Canadian residents will be charged applicable taxes. Offer not valid in Quebec. This offer is limited to one order per household. Not valid for current subscribers to Harlequin Blaze books. All orders subject to credit approval. Credit or debit balances in a customer's account(s) may be offset by any other outstanding balance owed by or to the customer. Please allow 4 to 6 weeks for delivery. Offer available while quantities last.

Your Privacy—The Harlequin® Reader Service is committed to protecting your privacy. Our Privacy Policy is available online at www.ReaderService.com or upon request from the Harlequin Reader Service.

We make a portion of our mailing list available to reputable third parties that offer products we believe may interest you. If you prefer that we not exchange your name with third parties, or if you wish to clarify or modify your communication preferences, please visit us at www.ReaderService.com/consumerschoice or write to us at Harlequin Reader Service Preference Service, P.O. Box 9062, Buffalo, NY 14269. Include your complete name and address.

HB13R2

SPECIAL EXCERPT FROM

HARLEQUIN®

Blaze®

Kate Hoffmann starts a new chapter in her
beloved miniseries with the New Zealand
Quinns—Rogan, Ryan and the namesake of the
April 2014 release

The Mighty Quinns: Malcolm

Mal is the protector of his family, and right now
they need protection from nosy reporters.
Like Amy Engalls. She wants a story...unless he
can give her something better....

Amy could barely catch her breath. It was as if she was tumbling
down a mountainside and she couldn't gain a foothold. But
now that she'd gained momentum, she didn't want to stop.

Mal was the kind of guy she could only dream about
having—handsome, charming, fearless. And now, she'd been
handed the chance to be with him, to experience something
she might never find in her life again. Sure, she'd had lovers in
the past, but they'd never made her feel wild and uninhibited.
Just once, she wanted to be with a man who could make her
heart pound and her body ache.

Just a week ago, she'd been curled up on her sofa in her
Brooklyn flat, eating a pint of cherry chocolate-chip ice cream

and watching romantic comedies. That had been her life, waiting for Mr. Right. Well, it was time to stop waiting. She'd found Mr. Right Now here on the beach in New Zealand.

This wouldn't be about love or even affection. It would be about pure, unadulterated passion. This would be the adventure she'd never been brave enough to take. She wasn't about to pass this opportunity by. If she couldn't leave New Zealand with a story, then she'd leave with a damn good memory.

At the bedroom door, Mal stopped. He grabbed her hands and pinned them above her head, searching her gaze. "Are you sure this is what you want?" he murmured, pressing his hips against hers.

The quilt fell away, leaving Amy dressed only in her underwear. She could feel his desire beneath the faded fabric of his jeans—he was already completely aroused. Amy wanted to touch him there, to smooth her fingers over the hard ridge of his erection. She could be bold, too. "Yes," she said, pushing back with her body.

He kissed her again, his lips and tongue demanding a response. She did her best to match his intensity, and when he groaned, Amy knew that *she* was exactly what he wanted.

**Pick up THE MIGHTY QUINNS: MALCOLM
by Kate Hoffmann, available March 18
wherever you buy Harlequin® Blaze® books.**

When opposites attract, sparks fly!

What do you get when you bring together a hot navy SEAL—aka Aiden Masters—who's addicted to rules, and a sexy free spirit like Sage Taylor, who sets out to break every rule she can? Sparks!

Don't miss the next chapter of the Uniformly Hot! miniseries

A SEAL's Kiss

by *USA TODAY* bestselling author
Tawny Weber!

Available March 18, 2014,
wherever you buy Harlequin Blaze books.

There is only one rule in
the game of seduction:
don't fall in love!

How much skimpy lingerie does it take to seduce
a billionaire? Clothing designer Allie McDonald
isn't sure, but her lakeside catch-and-release plan
backfires when sexy Jonas Meyer hooks her instead!

Don't miss

Nothing to Hide

by reader favorite author
Isabel Sharpe

Available March 18, 2014,
wherever you buy Harlequin Blaze books.